I0658281

Published by CollinRichard Publishing

First Edition May 2015

Printed in the United States of America

ISBN: 978-0996400602

DEDICATION

*This book is dedicated to a few very special people in my life. To my dear friend; the one that has always had my back and listened while
I dreamt out loud; Shaunta.*

To my mother, Terry, and Auntie Cynthia; without you I would have never known nor challenged what it is to be Determined, Dedicated or Motivated.

Last, but not least, to my husband, Richard, and son, Collin. I can't even begin to put words on paper that would or could describe how much I love you two.

ACKNOWLEDGMENTS

This past year has been a wonderful journey and I've been blessed to share it with so many people. I want to thank each and every one of you for your support and words of encouragement and collaboration which promoted me to begin this journey.

To Mrs. Reed, for all of your expertise and guidance. I appreciated all of your patience and willingness to answer all of my million and two questions before, during and after I started this journey.

To all of my new supporters, I hope you enjoy Lauren's story. I can assure you there is more to come, so stay tuned!

www.donnitalachey.com

CHAPTER ONE

It was a wicked night and the vehicle reverberated with storm warnings and damage reports blaring from the radio. Even though the sounds were reminiscent of that storm so long ago, Lauren did not hear them.

What the hell have I done? she mentally shrieked at herself. *What the fucking hell have I done?*

She pounded the steering wheel with both gloved fists and in return, it veered toward the oncoming lane. Something in her subconscious pulled it back, but over-corrected and the tires clacked over the warning grooves in the road's shoulder.

She gasped for air; unconsciously she had been holding her breath. It was as if the very function of breathing detracted from her ability to think. *How in the hell did I not see this coming? I'm smart...I'm ambitious and my bullshit radar is operating on overload. How in the fucking hell did this happen?*

5

Lies...is there a lie I can come up and cover with? Could he be too sick to catch on? Can I bullshit the doctors into keeping it from him?

And then there's my baby...my dear, sweet little boy. What will this do to him? What do I tell him when he's old enough to understand? What the fuck was I thinking? I knew better than this. It's not like I don't have enough shit on my plate right now...I had to add more and did it personally!

Tears of anger and self-loathing exploded and further blurred her ability to see in the raging storm. In that one moment she wished God would calmly reach down and pluck her from where she sat...that He would take her into His loving, forgiving arms and save her the Hell that lay before her. But that would be too easy. She bought her ticket to Hell and now she had to ride it out.

All those years of legal training; of looking for back doors and only letting people see the angles she wanted them to see. In this moment, all that had abandoned her and for agonizing minutes she felt the excruciating tension her clients must feel as they await the jury's verdict. She knew now what it was like to be

6

a tiny rabbit, cowering in a cage whose door she had inadvertently tripped shut. She was trapped. She was the prey; and she had sprung the damned trap on herself!

"Eeeeeeerrrrgggghhhhhh!" she screamed inside the empty vehicle, again pounding the wheel. A fresh explosion of frustrated, frightened tears clouded the view. In that single moment she heard the verdict being announced against her. In that single moment, God and jury, her husband and son announced her sentence. She rubbed her eyes with the leather glove and it was when she again squinted through tears that she saw her sentence.

Two bright lights were advancing on her; two bright lights borne by the Devil himself...and they were coming straight at her! "Noooooooooooooooo..." she screamed. Lightning flashed and that was her last conscious thought.

* * *

Rain pattered against the mullioned windows and fingers of shrubbery leaned against their fragile glass in a desperate effort to fend off the wind. The hand-blown hurricane style lamp watched from its table before the window, the effect casting wild shadows on the parquet flooring of the foyer.

Monica had retreated from the gale to the relative safety and comfort of the family room. The flat screen on the wall over the fireplace fed explosive live camera shots from the storm's damage into the room, making her shudder and supremely glad she had nothing on her calendar that evening.

Raspberry Pink the nail polish bottle read on its label. Monica, who was definitely a flashing red sort of woman, had decided on a whim to try a new look. Raspberry pink beckoned from the cosmetic counter and she had snatched it up, along with matching lipstick. She sat sideways on the tufted sofa, a tray holding manicure implements and the tiny bottle of raspberry pink balanced on the cushion next to her. Monica frowned slightly, recalling the price on that little bottle and resolved next time to just have a gallon of red enamel mixed up at Home Depot; enough to last a lifetime.

She had just finished the first coat when her cell phone vibrated with its night voice from the cherry coffee table.

Damn! she cursed to herself. She was forever the victim of bad timing. She quickly set the bottle on the tray and gingerly reached with splayed fingers to pick up the cell. It almost went to voice mail before she managed to bend her fingertip broad enough to tap the answering button.

"Yes... hello?" she answered in an impatient voice. She leaned back against the cushions, expecting Lauren's familiar voice to launch into a re-telling of today's exploits.

"Is this Monica Hammond?" asked the unknown voice on the line.

Monica sat up a bit, instantly alert. Something was wrong; she felt it.

"Who wants to know?" she responded, her voice lilting upwards as would a child, preparing for terrifying words. Her voice was instantly on the defensive. More pictures of the storm's victims flashed from the massive screen on the wall. The red ticker ran across the bottom of the screen; *BREAKING NEWS* it read. Her subconscious saw a black SUV rolled on its side, red lights from emergency vehicles gathered around it.

"Ms. Hammond, this is the Metropolitan Police Department."

Oh, God! Who is it? What's happened? Why the fuck are they calling me? She couldn't breathe and her brain was shutting down, preparing for what was to come. She said nothing as her hand began to shake.

"Ms. Hammond, are you there?" came the voice again.

"Yes, she whispered after long moments.

"Ms. Hammond, are you acquainted with a woman named Lauren Reynolds? We've found your number on her phone."

Monica had already begun to panic, tears building in her terror-filled eyes. "Yes," she whispered again, this time cowering against the bad news she knew was coming. "What is it? What's wrong?"

The voice at the other end was solemn and formal, calmly relaying the news it had been told to tell.

"Noooooooooo…." moaned Monica in a thin, tortured voice that came from the back of her throat.

The cell dropped from the smeared grip. Raspberry pink now lay on its side, its thin trail across the sofa cushions now pooling on the white carpet below.

CHAPTER TWO

Four years earlier

Thunder rolled in the distance while drops of rain began to pummel the office window. Lauren cursed under her breath, "Damn! It's starting to rain," while automatically reaching for the phone to check for messages. She dropped onto the office sofa, her long, sleek legs folding beneath her as her Dolce & Gabanna pumps slid to the oriental carpet. Lauren threw her head back against the cushion and looked skyward. "Not a single freakin' invitation and here it is after ten o'clock on a Friday night! Is *this* what you call the price of success?"

She took a moment to admire the symbols of success about her. This was her office and she was a partner in one of the most prestigious law firms in the state; not to mention their only female partner. The other partners lurked in darkly paneled offices behind massive desks. She, on the other hand, had chosen glass and sleek granite furniture with cream, upholstered side chairs and sofa. She was determined to draw spotlights on her success. At times she even allowed herself to think about a possible step into the political arena.

Everything Lauren did dripped of class. From her perfectly manicured appearance to the cream Escalade she drove, she had always been patient. She never settled but waited and plotted until she could have the best. She held herself above the others and they often resented her female arrogance. She didn't give a shit, though...it was her due. She paid a high price to get here and now she deserved the best money, or power, could buy. She was living her dream.

She executed a quick email, grabbed her handbag and headed out of the office and down the elevator for the subterranean parking garage. Such a strange world that was; dimly lit and almost vacant at this hour. The concrete was stained with oil and rubber tire prints yet it provided a shelter from the growing storm outside.

Lauren stood there momentarily, trying to remember why her Porsche wasn't in its usual spot. She slapped her palm against her temple as she remembered she had driven the Escalade this morning after hearing the weather forecast. It was too large for her reserved space so she'd had to park a level lower in open parking.

She opted for the staircase over the elevator and picked her way carefully around the oil stains until the Escalade stood before her, its cream exterior gleaming in the dim light like a knight in shining armor. She welcomed the soft leather seat and threw her handbag onto the passenger side.

The rain had turned to snow as she pulled into the street, the headlights picking out the white curtain and making her shiver. *Times like this I want a fuckin' man handy* she thought to herself. Defiantly she sped up the on ramp and onto the expressway, preparing for her normal 30-minute commute. She hadn't gotten far before the horizon filled with strobing red lights and sirens were approaching from behind her in the whiteout mess. *I'd better get the hell off here,* she thought and pulled onto the shoulder where she could get around the clogging traffic and off the expressway.

Lauren masterfully steered the huge SUV through the city streets and headed for River Road. It hugged the riverbank from the city lights and eventually opened out into the country amidst the equine estates of old money. Lauren was relaxed against the plush upholstery, tapping the sound system to bring on her favorite Pandora playlist. The music reverberated against the snow-covered windows and she tapped her free foot.

The Escalade had just crossed an old bridge when it began to sputter and a strobe of dashboard lights flashed warnings. "What the fuck?" Lauren spat out loud. The vehicle jerked and she barely had enough power to coast onto the shoulder of the road. Just as suddenly the engine died completely and she was left in the frigid darkness, alone on this seldom-used road.

"Oh, no....you're not going to quit on me now!" she said to no one in particular. "This is *not* how things work for me!" She reached for her handbag in the black interior and heard a number of items hit the floor as it tipped out of her reach. Infuriated, she slammed up the center console and armrests out of the way and leaned forward into the other seat to feel the floor for her cell. It was nowhere to be found. "Damn!" she cursed aloud. Somehow it made her feel better to make noise; it made her feel less vulnerable.

Calm your ass down, Lauren she thought to herself. *What makes sense to do right now?* She knew Aaron; her husband of seven years and legal partner in the firm would be pissed. Their life at home differed little from the polite distance they maintained at the office, but he still kept close tabs on her. It occurred to her from time to time that Aaron might be keeping someone on the side and that he tracked Lauren's coming and goings not so much because he cared, but because he didn't want to get caught.

This is no time to worry about that crap, she told herself. *I'm stuck in the middle of nowhere without a phone and this damn storm is not letting up soon. I'm cold and hungry. Worse than that—I gotta pee!*

She hugged her leather coat around her more tightly, turning up the collar and tried not to break down. It was times like this, when she was out of her element and at the mercy of something bigger than herself that she thought back to her childhood beneath the searing Texas skies. She had felt so much more relaxed then but even though it was home, she still longed to escape. She thought she was too big for that dusty little town; that she was intended for fame. She was willing to work hard and do whatever it took and so when the scholarship came through for Harvard, she was on the first bus out of town. She never looked back. *Damn, I wish I had a little of that sun right now* she thought to herself.

Beginning to panic a little, she got to her knees and bent so her ass was in the air and her arms had better searching reach on the passenger floor. That's exactly how the headlights from the approaching car caught her; her skirt hiked up and one long, slinky leg in a Dolce heel extended into the air behind her.

A tap on her car window startled her, causing her to jerk upright and hit her head on the rear view mirror. "Damn!" she cursed, looking around and quickly pulling her skirt downward. The snow had formed a layer over the window and a man's hand was sweeping open a path on the glass next to her face. The next thing she saw was a strong chin and two hands cupped against the glass, dark eyes peering right at her.

"Lauren? Lauren Reynolds? Is that you?"

Startled that the eyes knew her name, Lauren jerked backward, more than a bit alarmed.

"Lauren, it's me. Justin...from the firm." He was tapping now and motioning for her to roll down the window.

Justin? she thought, trying to gather her thoughts. "Justin? Justin Wilder? Is that you?" Her voice rose in delight as she forgot herself and recognized the handsome paralegal she had eyeballed more than once as he walked through the offices. *You're married* she'd told herself and knew that lady partners did not dip into the subordinate's pool, no matter how hot he looked or how sharp his mind. It did not serve well to encourage those you stepped on to get where you were going.

Naturally when the power was gone, so were the windows so Lauren simply opened the door. "Justin? Thank you for stopping. The car quit, I don't know what's wrong but I have no power."

He stood there, snowy rain catching glimmers of light from the beams of his car, and smiled. Lauren felt her tummy quiver and wondered briefly how it came that she had never noticed the dimple in his chin. He took the door in hand and opened it broadly, motioning her. "Here, slide over and let me give it a try," he said

18

as he gently pushed her hip to slide her into the passenger seat. She was all legs and stiletto heels as she tumbled over, at the same time wondering why the insinuation that he could start a car better than she, didn't piss her off.

Lauren got a whiff of his cologne as he slid behind the wheel, his gloved hand reaching to turn the key. She felt a quickening below as she realized how erotic a man's gloved hand could be. Not even a warning light came on now—it was completely dead. "Let me have a quick look," he said and left to pop the hood and look beneath. Lauren always wondered what it was that men thought they would see. It seemed to be sort of a ritualistic obligation – to look under the car hood. *There isn't a light or a tool within walking distance; what does he expect to do?* She barely had the thought out when the door whished open again and he leaned inside.

"It's dead," he announced and she bit her smartass response. "Probably the battery or something in the electrical but I don't have a jumper in my car and it's too dark to do anything. Did you call for help?"

Again she bit her lip to avoid a snarky remark and instead said, "No cell. Lost it somewhere between the office and here. It might be on the floor here; that's what I was looking for when you showed up."

She wondered why he was grinning at that remark and then remembered that she'd been ass up to the window when he looked in. She could tell by the look in his appreciative eyes that he, like her, was also trying not to say the obvious.

"Well, how about you grab what you *can* find there in the dark and come get into my car. It may not be a Caddy but at least it's warm and running. You look frozen," he offered. She started to hesitate; to ask him to call a wrecker from his cell, but thought better of it and dutifully clambered out of her dead vehicle.

A moment later she was in his car and the smell of his aftershave was far stronger here. He pushed away a couple of empty paper coffee cups and said, "Buckle up, the roads are slick." With that he put it into gear and started slowly down the road. He smoothly reached to flip on the Mustang's seat warmer and soon Lauren's thighs began to get hot. She wasn't sure if it was the seat or the driver, but it felt unfamiliar and very, very good.

"You're making me hot," she said without thinking.

He smiled at this and reached to flip the button back off for the seat warmer. "I'm assuming you mean the seat..." he said in a low voice but the insinuation hung heavily in the air between them.

Lauren struggled to come up with small talk. "So, how long have you been with Anderson & Anderson?" she began, not even sure if she was interested in anything other than hearing his sexy voice so nearby. As long as she stuck to business, it was probably safe.

CHAPTER THREE

"So where are we headed?" Justin asked.

"What do you mean?" Lauren could feel her bullshit radar kick in. She hadn't gotten to where she was by being a soft, submissive female who overlooked the subtleties of conversation. She had a reputation for being insightful and hard-nosed when it came to representing her clients…and herself.

Justin's profile in the dashboard lights reflected his surprise. "Well, I wondered where you wanted to go. Were you headed home?"

Lauren flushed at the abruptness of her response and eased back a bit. "Sorry, it's hard to turn off the business thinking even though it's late at night."

"I get it," he said. "You know, Lauren, I *do* understand and this might be a bit awkward for you but I have to ask. Why didn't you just call your husband to come and get you?"

"I told you. My cell is missing. I was just trying to decide a game plan when you showed up." She fidgeted and then burst out, "Look, Justin. I know this is a lot to ask but I'm helpless without a phone and until I locate mine, I'd like to go by the office and pick up the spare one I keep in my desk."

"Your spare phone?" he questioned.

"Well, you never know when yours can get picked up or take a swim in the toilet, you know?" she asked in a tentative voice. For some reason she wanted him to agree that her obsessive attention to avoiding disasters was perfectly normal.

Justin chuckled; that deep, resonating sound that came from somewhere in that *very* male chest. "I suppose I do. Would you like to go by the office?" he offered.

"Oh, would you? I know the roads are shit but it would be great. I mean, we have no idea whether we can even get into the office tomorrow after this mess keeps up through the night, you know?"

"No problem at all. I'd be happy to," he responded and his turn signal came on to prove it.

She was rummaging through her Marc Jacobs handbag one last time when suddenly her hand closed around her cell phone. *Shit!* she thought. *Why didn't I find it before?* She opened her mouth to say something and then it caught in her throat as she turned to see his strong profile. Deftly, she flipped the phone to silent and then took out a Kleenex as subterfuge for digging in her bag. Hadn't she asked God for an invitation tonight? Here he was, sitting right next to her, and in the role of her rescuer. How much better could it get? Screw Aaron and his other women.

They soon arrived at the office and Justin pulled in to the parking garage. "Let me come up with you," he said and his tone didn't suggest she had any options.

As they entered her office, Lauren signaled toward the chair. "Have a seat. I'll get it and be right with you," as she headed toward her desk.

Justin sat as invited and then looked around with a low whistle. "So, this is what it feels like to be on top," he said softly.

Lauren's back was to him at that moment and she stiffened. *Could he be referring to bed?* "Excuse me?" she asked as she turned around.

"All of this," he motioned around the room with his hand and she noted there were no rings. "This is what I have to look forward to?"

She studied his face to see if he was teasing her. "It's not that easy," she said and then regretted sounding so condescending. "Do you plan to go on to law school?"

He looked surprised. "Of course. Did you think I was content to be a paralegal for the rest of my life?" His brow was furrowed.

Lauren paused and decided to be completely truthful. "I really never gave it thought, to tell you the truth. I barely knew who you were."

"Yeah, I get that," he sighed. "It's always a matter of position."

She was startled again and wondered why she kept reading innuendo into everything he said. *Could be because it's been so damned long since I got laid,* she

25

thought to herself. She paused a moment and thought, *just how long has it been?* She couldn't immediately recall and that alone made it too damned long. However, her prospects were looking up she decided, looking at Justin relaxed in the side chair, his long legs splayed outward and apart like a tiger who was surveying the landscape. She wondered what it would be like to be pinned beneath those legs and suddenly felt a rush of moistness between her own.

Covering, she prompted, "Got the phone. Ready?"

He nodded and with the supple muscles of an athlete stood effortlessly and stepped back to let her pass. "So, where may I drop you?" he asked. Both were very aware of one another in that moment, and equally aware that she now had a phone and could call her husband...but chose not to.

"How about a drink?" she suggested. His smile answered and soon they were back in his Mustang and cruising the back streets of town.

Shortly they pulled up to a drive and he turned in, causing Lauren's brow to rise. "Where are we going?" she asked.

"Well, perhaps it has escaped your attention," he said wryly, "but the bars closed long ago. It's after two a.m."

She drew in her breath. "No! Actually I hadn't. It's just that time…" her voice trailed off as they pulled up to a low-roofed, neo-eclectic home surrounded with the woods. It was dark inside as she could see through the floor-to-ceiling windows that banked a large, walkout deck beneath the trees. Branches were hanging low, weighted by the ice that had begun to crust upon them.

In one smooth move, Justin was out of the car and at her side, opening her door. "Milady…" he mocked with a smile and a sweep of his arm, holding out his hand to help her. "Be careful, it's slick," he said just as her spike heel hit the ice and she felt herself falling backwards.

Justin caught her and then scooped her up into his arms. "I'd better carry you. You'll never get inside alive in those things," he said, eyeing her $900 shoes.

At the front door he paused and tapped a keypad lock next to the frame. Nothing happened. "Uh, oh…, that's bad," he said, frowning and setting her down on the covered tile of the porch.

"What?" she asked.

"No power," he said, tipping over a statue and retrieving a key hidden beneath. "The backup generator isn't working either, it appears."

"How ingenious of you to hide a key beneath the statue," she said. She couldn't resist, flustered after feeling his strong arm against her hosiery-clad thighs.

"It's not what you think," he said and turned back toward his car. He popped the hood of the Mustang and removed a slender black box that was fastened to the inside of the hood. Using the key, he unlocked the box and removed yet another key and this was what he used to unlock the front door. "It's my backup key," he explained as the door slid open.

Why doesn't he just carry it on his keychain? she mused, but said aloud, "Well, I suppose no burglar would ever consider simply taking a crow bar to one of those windows," she pointed with her hand.

"It's more than a key, Lauren. When the power comes back on, I'll show you. In the meantime, I just happen to have a bottle of rare Chablis breathing on the bar. I was headed to the store for some cheese when I came across you," he explained.

"Yes, and I'm really glad you did," she said softly, watching his face to get a read on what he was thinking.

"Not as glad as I," he responded, smiling gently. "Here, let me take those things," he held out his hands and once again she wondered whether he intended her to strip, there and then. "Your coat and purse," he said, nodding again toward her. "You're wet and need to get dried and warm," he said, his voice held genuine care.

She obediently slid out of the leather trencher and handed it to him. She rubbed her arms and in three seconds she felt a huge, soft robe being settled over her shoulders. "You'd better get out of all that," he voice was right behind her. "You're taking a chill. Why don't you step into the room behind you and I'll get you that wine." She looked up at him with a sidelong glance and saw he was sincere and his dark eyes held compassion. She had never encountered a man who

29

made her feel this way; so coddled and cared about. Who was he?

She nodded and found a bathroom of spotless white tile that glowed in the lightning from the storm. There was a huge soaking tub and she couldn't resist. She turned on the tap and steaming water filled it. Just as she was about to disrobe, there was a tap on the door. She opened it, still dressed.

"I thought you might need these," Justin said softly, holding out a lighted candle and a goblet of wine. "Take your time. We have the rest of the night," he murmured and closed the door as he left.

Lauren stood there long moments wondering what he had meant. Using the candle he'd brought, she lit three others that were sitting on the edge of the tub. Briefly she wondered whether it was his habit to take candle-lit baths and decided it wasn't worth contemplating because it would ruin the mood.

She took a sip of the wine, her clothes hit the floor and she sank into the steaming water. She closed her eyes and lay back, running her hands over her thighs with the luxury of the moment. She thought of Justin, just outside that unlocked door and suddenly felt another rush of heat inside herself. Using the bar of soap, she lavishly soaped her legs and then slid her own hand up between and just inside herself. She couldn't bring herself to fondle the tender skin; that job was reserved for someone else. She did dream about it, though, and slowly and sensuously washed away the evidence.

When the water cooled, she climbed out regretfully and donned the robe, pulling the sash tightly about her waist. It hung hugely on her, but somehow it made her look all the more fragile and helpless she thought as she considered herself in the mirror. *I wonder if he likes the helpless type?* she mused, as she headed for the door. *I'm his boss, for God's sake. Helpless could help level the playing field.*

She opened it and there stood Justin in the middle of the living room. He was dressed only in a pair of lounge pants, his magnificent body outlined against the dim glow of a fire he had laid.

"I thought we were only stopping for a drink," she said in a very soft, melodic voice.

"We were," he agreed after a long moment. He came toward her then, his hand held out to take hers as he led her to the sofa and eased her down onto it. "But then why are you in such a hurry to go? It's a nightmare out there," he pointed over his shoulder to the sleet biting the huge glass windows. "I have an extra bedroom for you and besides...this will give us a chance to talk. You may work on Saturdays, but I don't. Are you hungry?"

She nodded but they both knew it wasn't food she wanted. "Do you want to use my landline to call your husband?" he asked in a quiet voice. This time she shook her head *no*. He said nothing more but lifted his own goblet of wine and sat down beside her, his eyes searching the opening of the robe. Lauren felt her nipples tingle and she longed to throw open the robe and feed him...but she sat there demurely, waiting to see what his next move would be. It came quickly, and when it did, it was not what she expected.

CHAPTER FOUR

"Is that an authentic Jackson Pollock?" Lauren asked, looking for some way to relieve the sexual tension in the room.

"An investment," he said simply.

"How did you..." she wanted to ask but didn't quite know how to without being nosy. This man did not live on a paralegal's meager salary.

"Family," he answered simply. That said it all.

Having scrapped her way to where she was now, Lauren was always amazed how people who were born to money regarded it. She may as well have been referring to a Precious Moments figurine instead of the priceless Pollock painting she was now looking at. Justin was completely casual and offered no bragging comments whatsoever.

"I see. Where do they..." she ventured again.

33

"Upstate. My brother is on the west coast. I'm the eldest and it's expected I follow in the family footsteps. I wanted medicine but Father was persistent and eventually I gave in to make him happy. When he's no longer around to give me a hard time, I'll go back to med school. Anyway, the way I figure it, who better to practice malpractice law than a doctor to be, right?"

Lauren was agog at his casual attitude and didn't know whether to envy him or hold him in disdain.

"Things come easily for you, don't they?" she asked, barely masking her grassroots contempt.

"Not as easily as you might think, Lauren," he answered. "The problems are probably the same you've encountered. Mine just came with more zeros."

Again, that casual attitude. She wondered whether he had the heart of a good attorney. *Could he be a shark if he needed to?* He seemed to read her mind.

"It's all perspective, Lauren. I can choose to take life oh so seriously and lose sight of the big picture. Or..." he sipped his wine, "I can save the guns for the battle and live in peace in the meantime."

34

He made it sound so simple and she leaned back to think about this when there was an enormous crash coming from one end of the house.

Justin leapt up from the sofa and indicated with a hand movement for her to stay put. He disappeared through a dark doorway and she heard him curse. He soon reappeared and there was a frown on his face.

"Tree came through the window in the guest room," he said. "No point calling anyone tonight. You'll have to bunk in my room, I'm afraid. I'll take the sofa."

"Oh, I don't mind the sofa," Lauren began. "I've slept on my share in my lifetime," and then stopped when she realized how that sounded. "I mean…"

"Don't sweat it, Lauren. I won't compromise your privacy and I won't sleep in the bed while knowing you're on the sofa, so give it up. Anyway, I can keep a better eye on your welfare if I know you're safely in the end of the house where there are no overhanging trees."

The matter seemed settled and she marveled at how easily he dealt with something that would have thrown her for days. *Maybe that's what having money all your life does for you. You always know you have it covered.*

There was a lesson to be learned in that. She realized that she was not the only thing he wanted vantage to protect. There was, after all, that Pollock on the wall and probably more treasures she simply hadn't seen yet. She felt humbled. She remembered the triumph she'd felt when she'd bought her first Marc Jacobs handbag. She had sported it everywhere and even bought a wardrobe to match it instead of the other way around. Here was Justin, a fortune hanging on the wall and he was as casual as if it were a paint-by-number. She realized then that the real secret in having money was that no one else should realize it. But they did...they always did.

He set his wine glass down on the table and held out his hand. "Come on, come with me," and she dutifully arose and went with him. They entered another dark room and it smelled of his cologne. She knew that no matter how long she lived; she would always remember how he smelled.

Justin left her standing momentarily while he appropriated a candle from one of the other rooms. He used it to light a path to the bed and went ahead of her to pull back the covers. "In you go," he said, motioning her to lie down. She sat on the edge of the bed, perplexed.

"Are you planning to sleep in that thing?" he asked, eyeing the robe.

"Well, I don't seem to have anything else at the moment," she started.

"You have what God gave you," he said and took her hand long enough to bring her back to standing. He set the candle on the nightstand and as he looked her directly in her deep eyes, he slowly slid his hand forward and with excruciating tenderness, untied the robe's sash and slid the robe off her shoulders to pool on the carpet. He worshipped her with his eyes for long moments. His hand ventured forward again, as if to cup her full breast with reverence, but at the last moment he remembered himself and with a sigh of regret, motioned to the bed. "Better get in there before I forget how I was brought up to treat a woman."

Lauren felt a keen disappointment. A married woman who initiated was shameless; a man who approached a married woman couldn't help himself and therefore she was exonerated. At least that's how it worked in the law of Lauren.

She looked at him, a glimmer in her eye and he knew the disappointment she was feeling. "You're making me hot," she said again softly. "But this time there's no button to turn it off."

Justin looked down at her from his towering height and then slowly moved one man-sized hand forward and let his fingers trail in the hair of her womanhood. Lauren started with a shock at his brazen touch. Her breath expelled and unconsciously her hips tilted forward to seek him further. He petted her there, tracing the perimeter of her hairline with his long index finger and then while using his other hand to cup her ass, pushed that finger into her clitoris. Lauren swooned and her eyes closed as she fell back against the bed, arms outstretched to pull him down to her. *To hell with propriety* she thought, burning with desire for him.

Lauren's hand came up now and she traced the outline of his massive penis through the fabric of his lounge pants. It was easy to find, even in the darkness. There was no mistaking the erection or the size. He moaned but grabbed her hand at the wrist and firmly pushed it back, using his other hand to draw the comforter over the top of her.

"I'm saving us both, Lauren," he whispered. "You have no idea how badly I want you," he said, "but you also have no idea how much you'll regret it in the morning."

With this, he turned with athletic grace and after only a momentary pause of regret; he left the room and closed the door softly.

Lauren was left with her morals tarnished, but her honor intact. With a sigh, she rolled over and hugged his pillow against her womanhood. *We'll see about this tomorrow,* she thought. She never questioned that there would be an opportunity tomorrow.

* * *

A few minutes later the bedroom door opened. Justin stood there, looking at her. "I'm leaving the door open so you get some heat from the fireplace," he said.

"Is that the only reason?" Lauren answered in a soft voice.

"It's the only one I can live with right now," he replied.

"I can think of another one," she murmured.

"They say you always win your case," Justin's voice was deep and husky.

"They're right," she replied.

CHAPTER FIVE

Lauren did not want to talk to her husband. In fact, she wanted to pretend he did not even exist. When she awakened the next morning the sky was granite gray and there was a layer of ice everywhere she looked. She snaked her cell out of her purse and texted him.

Aaron, the Escalade broke down and someone from the firm happened by and saw me. Am sheltering from the storm there. Left my charger in the car so I hope this message gets through. Don't worry – am just fine. Be home as soon as I can.

She waited a few minutes and soon a response came.

Okay.

She lay there, her face burning with anger. *Aaron doesn't even give a fuck where I am – why did I bother?* She knew why she bothered. It wasn't because she felt a strong sense of obligation to her husband; it was because she wanted a window of time with Justin—a window that no one would question.

She tagged the robe and went into the living room. Justin was still asleep on the sofa, the fireplace poker on the carpet beside him. He'd evidently been up most of the night tending the flames to keep the house warm.

Lauren found the kitchen and set about scouting out something to eat and the coffee. She realized she'd only had a few sips of wine the night before and she was famished. Before long she was scrambling eggs; luckily Justin's stove was gas and there were matches to light the burners. Coffee would be crude; an improvised pot of boiling water poured over a strainer with coffee grounds directly into two mugs.

She felt, rather than heard, Justin coming up behind her. His voice was soft so as not to startle her and it came from no more than four inches above her head.

"That smells wonderful...enough for two?"

"Of course," she smiled. "No telling how long the power will be off. We need to eat what's in the fridge first so you don't lose it.

"Don't worry," he said. "Now that it's daylight, I'll head outside and figure out why the generator didn't kick in. We'll have power in no time...at least *we* will."

Why was it that the thought of being marooned in this icy world with only Justin made her wet? Two days ago she would have been outraged to think she would be relying on a paralegal for her survival and here she was, wanting to feel him inside her. *What has happened to me?*

Lauren made two plates and set them on the snack bar at the end of the island. She'd found a bowl of fruit and sliced two oranges to frame the eggs. She found cloth napkins and some beautiful tableware and even added a flower she'd spied in a bouquet in the foyer. The effect was charming, particularly in contrast to the silvery ice world outside the windows.

Justin still wore the lounge pants and seemed very comfortable. She selfishly imagined for a few moments what it would be like to be married to him, to enjoy every morning together just like this before they'd set off to work. She would insist he work with her directly and at lunch they would lock the door and make passionate love on the cream sofa in her office. She realized then he was speaking to her.

"What? I'm sorry, my mind was elsewhere," she hid her thoughts as her face flooded with color.

He smiled as if he knew her thoughts, but repeated himself. "I was just asking if you thought you should let your husband know where you are and call someone to pick up the Escalade? I do have a working phone, you know."

"Oh-oh…I forgot to mention. This morning I was in my handbag for something and believe it or not, found my main phone. I texted Aaron. As for the car, I'll call AAA and let them know where to pick it up. I doubt there's anyone moving in this mess, though. Have you heard anything about the weather?" she hurried through, hoping he wouldn't ask any more questions.

"You weren't planning on trying to get into the office today, were you?" he asked, a half smile on his face.

"Uhhh, no, no need to risk life and limb. It will all wait until Monday."

"Monday? Will you be staying through the weekend?" he asked, smiling more broadly.

Lauren looked at the floor, her thoughts racing. "Well, if you have no other plans, I thought I might... just to be on the safe side, you understand. Anyway, I have a case coming up and I've requested you to work with me on it," she lied through her teeth. Lauren always made it a practice to work alone. "We could go over my notes and talk about some strategy." She looked up at him to see his reaction and his smile was still there. "Can I stay?" she asked in a small voice.

He let her hang there a few moments, then looked back at his plate and said, "I think that's a superb idea as a matter of fact."

She allowed herself a breath of relief.

He went on, "My brother's wife left some clothes behind last time they visited. They might be a bit big on you but you'll find them in the box on the shelf of the closet. There should be something in there you can use...just for the weekend," he emphasized with an exaggerated tone. She could have kicked him.

Justin stood and walked over to the counter, depositing his plate in the dishwasher. "I'll be outside for a bit. Stay away from the room at the end of the hall. There's broken glass everywhere and I suspect a good deal of ice. I'll get the generator running and we'll have everything back to normal shortly." With that he left the kitchen and Lauren settled down to finish her breakfast...and plot.

* * *

Lauren found the box of clothes and there wasn't much there; just about what you might leave in the dryer and overlook in packing. They were considerably too large for her, but she found a t-shirt and Lycra yoga pants that weren't too bad. With a

46

devilish streak she left off her bra and the effect was definitely intriguing.

She left the bedroom just as lights popped on and the sound of a furnace fan began to whir. The LED lights on the electronics began blinking and Lauren almost felt a sense of regret. It would have been nice to keep warm next to Justin and this was just her style of camping.

He stomped in through the back door and called out, "Is that it? Everything on?" as though she would know. He came into the living room and saw her standing there in her makeshift outfit. "I see you found the clothes. You look...well...dry," he finished lamely but she caught his eyes on her breasts, outlined and sweet nipples erect against the t-shirt fabric.

"Oh, yes, everything appears to be just fine," she said slyly and went to the sofa. "Come and sit with me for a while and let's talk."

"Be there in a minute," he answered and disappeared into the bedroom. He emerged, dressed in jeans and a sweatshirt with a big "H" on the front. *God, but he's hot even in that ol' thing* Lauren couldn't help thinking. His hair was damp and she could smell soap from where she sat. There was nothing sexier than a cleanly showered man in tight jeans and a ratty sweatshirt she thought. *Unless it's a cleanly showered man naked and between my legs* she amended her thought.

"So, how did you sleep?" he inquired with a bit of a satirical tone to his voice.

"How do you think?" she countered in her best lawyerly manner.

"Probably very much like I did," he responded, looking at her breasts.

There was a silence between them as each struggled with the choice of small talk or simply throwing caution to the wind and ripping off their clothes.

"We can't," he said very quietly.

"Why?" she answered in a small, pleading voice.

"You're married. You're my boss. So many reasons," he answered.

"My marriage is a sham. I'm also a woman. Fuck the rest of the reasons," she countered.

"Your husband is also my boss," he said.

"You don't need a job. Look at this place," she verbally jousted. "Fuck Aaron! He's got others."

"I'd rather fuck you," he said with a growl. He stood suddenly and began pacing. "Don't you have any idea what's going through my head right now? Do you think I'm immune to you? Damn you for being who you are, Lauren. I've watched you for months! For months! I've had to sit there and pretend to read books while that pert little ass of yours walked right past me. I've smelled your woman scent when you leaned over the copier next to my desk. I had to ignore your nipples peeking through those tight white blouses you wear and believe me...they stand out when you're fired up. You're beautiful; you're smart as shit and you're bound for big things, Lauren. There's even talk around the office that someday you'll be in a position to help the firm, but from the capitol building."

"Where did you get that idea?" Lauren demanded, her radar suddenly triggered.

Justin hesitated a few moments, turning so his back was toward her, buying time. "Just here and there, you know...water cooler conversations."

Lauren's head tilted. She had learned over the years that it was not what people said, but how they behaved that told you the most. Obviously Justin wasn't going to offer any more details. That was okay. She would bide her time.

"Lauren?"

"Hmmm?" she tried to ignore the heat inside of her. It wouldn't do to lose her cool.

"Lauren, answer me this. How did you and Aaron meet?"

"In law school," she answered, puzzled. "He was a young law professor and I asked him for some private tutoring after hours. I was still shaking off the Texas dust and needed to be as polished as any Ivy League debutante. He had the aura, you know? That special something that people with money have?" He looked at her. "Justin, don't play dumb. You have it, too. You all do. You were just born with it, dammit. I wasn't.

50

I'm from a rough little town in the middle of nowhere and the biggest thing I have is a dream. That's all I've always had."

Justin was shaking his head. "No, you have, and you are much more than that, sweet Lauren. You don't even realize it, do you? You are what those debutantes can never hope to have. You are innocent, smart and determined. Their patina is polished into them from the day they're born. Their connections are deep, and crooked, and flawed. You're fresh and innocent. You are exactly what they need to get elected. Don't you see that?"

Lauren was thoughtful, remembering sitting in Aaron's lectures, admiring the way he took command of the room and kept everyone's interest. And later, after she had approached him for tutoring and they had become close, she took such secret pride in knowing she was sleeping with the professor and how jealous the other women in the room would be.

She had delighted in catching his eye as he spoke and pursing her lips into a feigned kiss. He would get flustered and stumble; completely out of character for him. It gave her a sort of power over him and it was then that she became aware of the kind of power an attractive woman could have...and use when it suited her. For her it was like a vampire's first bite of blood; she had the taste upon her tongue now and would close in for the kill any time it suited her.

"Justin, you're messing with my head. I'm here, trapped with you alone in your house and I've watched your eyes. Not only do they not stay on my face, there's a light in them every time you look at me. What kind of game are you playing here?" Lauren was getting fiery and this was always a sign for people to cut the crap and lay down their cards.

"I'm in love with you," Justin said very quietly, his back still to her and his words measured.

Lauren thought she misheard him. "Say that again?"

Justin swung around and strode to the sofa, pulling her to her feet and wrapping his long arms around her.

He tipped his chin and rested it on the top of her head. "You heard me. I'm in love with you."

She drew in her breath. "But you barely know me," she countered.

"No," he answered, "you barely know *me*."

Lauren stared up at him, not knowing what to say. Justin smiled and then cradled her face between his hands and slowly leaned downward to kiss her.

Startled, Lauren stiffened at first at the unexpected shock that went through her entire body when his lips touched hers. As the heat and texture of his tongue filled her mouth, she went limp and had he not been holding her, she might have collapsed. His tongue quested hers and circled it to skim the inside of her mouth.

Lauren's breathing quickened and her arms rose to encircle his neck, pulling him closer to her. Justin felt honest, trustworthy and loving; something she hadn't felt before with this depth. She suddenly had the mental impulse to crawl inside of him and let his body surround hers with a second skin. She wanted to be inside of him, and to have him inside of her.

Justin broke away suddenly, still holding her but now at an arm's length.

"What's wrong?" she gasped as cold air rushed to push away the warmth that had existed between them.

"We cannot do this, Lauren." His words were tortured and she could see his arousal despite the stiff denim of his jeans. She could feel herself aching and was having difficulty reconciling the passion of the previous moment with the sudden loss of contact. She felt like she was in a free fall.

"What's wrong?" she said again, this time in a whisper.

"I told you, I'm in love with you and there's nothing I would rather do than carry you to that bedroom right now and spend the day inside of you." His voice was ragged with need. "But eventually we would have to go back to our lives, to the people we were before this happened. They would know."

"Justin, do you think I can go back to the firm and never look at you again? Don't you think it's a little late for that kind of charade?"

"I should never have said anything," he looked at her, the torture apparent on his handsome face. "But I was lost in your nearness and reckless; perhaps we'll never be alone again."

Lauren could feel her panties were damp and there was a sweetly miserable ache low within her. She fought to breathe. "Justin?"

He turned slowly to face her again, "Yes?"

"For the record," she began, "I want you."

"I know," he said. "I know. And I want you."

"Could we just…" she began.

"No. It wouldn't stop there, you know that."

"I know," she said sadly, feeling the cold air enter her heart. She sat back down on the sofa and crawled into a fetal position, hugging a pillow into her throbbing womanhood."

Justin walked into the bedroom and slowly closed the door. Lauren sat miserably alone, tears streaming down her face until once again; she fell asleep before the warmth of the fire.

CHAPTER SIX

Lauren dreamed vividly as she slept. She had always been one who experienced colorful, real-life dreams; complete with color, sound, smells, tastes. Oftentimes she would awaken and have to lie there for some time, reconciling that it had only been a dream and that her waking world paled in comparison.

She was caught up in yet another one of those dreams. She could feel herself being lifted upward and sailing effortlessly through ribbons of air, then deposited on a cloud. Something was gently touching her, slipping her clothing off, one piece at a time and she could feel cool air caressing her nipples. In her dream, she slithered upward, reaching toward that delicious sensation with a need that bordered on frenzy. To her delight, the sensation moved downward, to her pussy. Something warm and moist was probing her.

Lauren's eyes wanted to open, but she desperately clung to the dream world, willing it not to end. She knew if she awakened, she would be desolated and alone again, as she was so often nowadays.

Her lids slid open slowly, despite her best efforts and it took a moment for her to adjust her eyes to even the dim light in the room. There was something moving close by, but oddly, she didn't want to move.

That woman's knowing gently told her now and she looked downward to find herself lying on a bed. Justin's broad chest was above her and then his head dove low and she could feel his strong fingers upon her womanhood. He cupped her with his huge hand and then as if pulling open the petals of a budding flower, his fingers opened her clit, tenderly and with a loving fascination. His touch was electric but did not compare with what came next.

As she watched, his face turned upward to look at her with haunted eyes, rich with need and desire. She felt herself opening her mouth, her head tossing back upon the pillow and gasping as the dream came true. Justin's face turned again and his lips fastened upon the tender folds of skin of her clit, sucking at them with gentle fascination but masculine intent.

Juices flooded her and she shivered as she saw his tongue probe her to sample her juices. He seemed to savor her, as if committing the taste of her to his memory. It was then that she realized that she was now in a cocoon of time that may never repeat itself.

She became instinctual; a pure feminine animal. Her hips rotated, that his tongue might linger upon spots that were most sensitive. The more she moved her hips, the further she slid downward, her legs opening wide to give him access. She could feel an orgasm launching, its stars beginning to fill her consciousness. Just as she was ready to burst, she felt his breath upon her, cooling her and bringing her back to earth. She moaned in disappointment and heard him chuckle in a whisper.

So close to release, Lauren's temper flared and she struggled to push away from him, but it was useless. Justin's arms were locked around her thighs as if in a wrestler's position. He looked at her with masculine delight and then bent backward so he could release his manhood upon her.

With a deep, smooth thrust, he was within her. Her breath caught in her throat and then her mind went back to that star-filled sky. He began a rhythm within her; one that transcended time and was instinctual as life itself. They began the dance of love; he leading and her rising and then pulling backward with her hips to receive him again.

As the music in their minds rose in volume and sped up, their thrusts became more frantic, more organic. Lauren cupped her own breasts and flailed beneath him, searching for skin contact for her tender nipples. Justin whispered words of love, of encouragement to her, kissing her mouth and her breasts in rotation.

"Cum for me sweetheart. It's you and I...no one else. This is our time, my darling. *Our* time. I'm in you and we will mix ourselves and become one. Cum for me, my darling Lauren."

She needed no encouragement. Her body reacted instinctually and just as she heard his moan of release, the stars returned and she felt transported by the spasms that emanated from within her and reached upward into those flashing skies. She cried out; frantic to hold on to the sensations, to Justin, to the creature they had become.

Justin lay upon her, his hand petting her tummy and down into the womanly fur he seemed to crave. He said only three words.

"I love you."

CHAPTER SEVEN

Justin's kiss made her want to live permanently in his bed, but the sight of his nakedness as he stood to dress made her want to die right then, before any other image could take its place in her memory.

He smiled and said, "C'mon, I'm hungry. Let me cook us something."

Jesus! He cooks, too? Lauren felt wiped out from all the events of the past day and while she would rather have gone to sleep, she nodded and joined him in her borrowed finery.

"What would m'lady like?" he teased, but promptly set about pulling out pans and ingredients and she knew he already had plans for what he was going to cook. She was content to let him surprise her.

"Set the table, please," he ordered and Lauren was struck by the fact that suddenly she was no longer in charge. It was a curious feeling; but in some ways felt more natural.

"Pour us a burgundy of your choice," Justin pointed at a small wine cooler in one wall.

"Smells delicious," Lauren complimented as the scent of mushrooms and garlic filled the room.

With a flourish, Justin eventually set two, beautifully arranged plates of *Coq au vin* on the table and handed her one of the wine glasses while he held the second. "To us," he toasted.

"To us," she echoed and wondered at the power of a toast to seal one's fate.

The magic of the day continued and after enjoying Justin's culinary skills, they crawled onto the sofa and Justin's touch on a remote brought a huge flat screen out of hiding. Lauren lay in his arms and they watched *Harvey* with Jimmy Stewart. It was a comforting, nurturing afternoon and Lauren fell asleep, her hair spilling out over Justin's protective chest.

Lauren later drew a bath and the two of them crawled in and luxuriated among the steaming bubbles and the touch of one another's skin. After emerging, Justin picked her up and took her back to his bed.

This time Justin stretched seconds into lifetimes. He kissed her every inch with tiny, sucking nibbles; dawdling upon her breasts and the soft skin just below her naval. Lauren writhed from left to right and as she did so. Justin positioned his fingers at the base of her pussy so she inadvertently, but deliciously screwed herself down upon them. She held his manhood in her hands, tracing the throbbing veins with light fingertips. Justin groaned with frustration; torn between languishing atop her beautiful body and taking her quickly to relieve the ache in his groin.

He opted for yet another choice and lifted her high into the air and then deposited her on her tummy. He moved to massage her feet and then took hold of her knees and shoved them forward beneath her. Now he straddled her and with her bottom high in the air, he entered her from the rear and Lauren screamed with the fulfillment.

In her head, there was only Justin; he filled her conscious world and her body craved his every touch. There was no guilt, no self-recrimination, no work, no Aaron.

Afterwards, Justin lay on his side and held her against him, pulling blankets to cover her bareness. His arm folded over her breasts and his hand cupped her womanhood possessively.

Both of them knew their time was at an end. Lauren could stay no longer without arousing suspicion; in fact, she had probably already stayed too long. The Escalade had been towed to the office parking lot and awaited her.

At some point, between her tears, they emerged from their cocoon and she began to dress in the clothes she had worn home from work. They felt stiff and lifeless after Justin's warmth. Lauren could not remember every feeling as desolate and sad as when Justin pulled up to the Escalade and she got out. He could not even kiss her goodbye, lest someone was watching. There was a whoosh of cold air as she closed his car door and picked her way over to the Escalade. Inside, she looked at him and his heart broke as he saw huge tears sliding down her cheeks.

Justin waited until she pulled away and she was only a dot in the distance, merging on to the expressway. With a curse, he slammed the Mustang into gear and spun it around several times in the parking lot before leaving, in another direction. He couldn't bear to see her taillights again.

CHAPTER EIGHT

Lauren arrived home and Aaron was gone. *It's just as well* she thought to herself. *I don't want to go through one of his depositions at this point.*

Lauren went into her bedroom. She and Aaron had been sleeping apart for some time now; ever since he had begun to walk the floors in the middle of the night. He had developed a habit of pacing from his study to the living room windows and after pausing to look outside, would retrace his steps. Sometimes he came back to bed within minutes, but as time went on, it became hours. Lauren wasn't able to sleep while this was going on. She lay in their bed, cold and alone, wondering what had his mind so occupied. He no longer touched her, so she eventually came to the conclusion that there were one or more women in his exterior life. His pacing probably had to do with what he planned to do about it. Once he finally returned to bed, he lay there very still, as if believing she was sleeping and not to disturb her. One such night Lauren reached for him tentatively in the belief that she still

67

had the power to reclaim him. He had taken her hand, firmly and briefly squeezed it before purposefully pushing it back to her side. Eventually, Lauren could take no more sleepless nights and when she moved into the guest suite, Aaron made no comment. They never even discussed it; Lauren could only assume doing so would force the issue for Aaron, so she kept her peace. After all, they were partners in the same law firm; such a divorce would make things sticky and could hurt the firm.

Lauren looked into her vanity mirror. *Odd, but I still look like myself* she thought to herself. *But I certainly don't feel like myself.* She stripped off her clothes and looked at herself in the full-length mirror. She turned and noticed a dark spot of her bottom. *Damn that Justin* she laughed to herself. *Leave it to him to mark his territory.* It made her feel warm inside to know he'd left a hickey on her. She turned on the shower but stood outside it until the steam had filled the room. She could still smell their combined scent upon herself and knew the moment she stepped into the shower, it would be gone.

Eventually, with an ache of longing, she stepped into the stream of water and soaped herself intimately, picturing Justin's hand in place of her own.

As she re-entered her bedroom, she bent to pick up her clothes. She separated her panties from the rest and put them to her nose; yes, his scent was still there as well. With sentimental reverence, she folded them and placed them in the corner of her drawer; never to be laundered.

Lauren knew there was rough water ahead. She had to pull herself together. Her life would be placed on hold; there was too much at the office to be done.

She put through a call and got the voice mail. Evidently, due to the weather, no one was in today. She took advantage of the break and took a long nap. She dreamed of Justin but a dark fog surrounded him and as she called to him, he turned his back and disappeared into that fog. Lauren awakened, tears on her cheeks. She slid her hand into her panties to touch the spot he'd left with his lips. It was a pitiful comfort in this situation, but the flesh and blood alternative was somewhere out there in the icy fog.

CHAPTER NINE

It was a day of confusion. There was havoc to be dealt with in rescheduling client appointments and court dates. Staff was strolling into the office in dribs and drabs. Evidently the power outage had taken out computer backups and even the tiny refrigerator in the conference room had dripped water and a partial box of summer popsicles someone had left in its micro freezer.

Lauren walked into the reception area and headed for her office with its glass walls, keeping her head down as she passed Justin's desk.

Aaron had come in very late and gone straight to his room; opening her door briefly to make sure she was in her bed. She feigned sleep so there would be no conversation and had left this morning before he arose. The more time she could put between her storm sheltering and the day-to-day realties of work, the better. He would get distracted and forget to interrogate, or so she prayed.

70

She sat at her desk, dropped her keys and her phone on its smooth surface and ran her fingers tentatively across its top. In many ways it reflected the tangents of her life. It was cold and unforgiving, just as the law she challenged, just as her future without Justin seemed. She buzzed her secretary, Betsy, for coffee and swung around to the credenza behind her desk to begin going through messages by the telephone.

"Your coffee," came a male voice and she swung around again to see Justin in her doorway, a sly smile on his face. Her face blanched as he entered, softly closing the door behind himself. "I intercepted your secretary in the kitchenette. Told her I had business with you and would bring it with me." He set the cup down on her desk and then looked at her with a sad smile, "What's the matter? Remember me?"

Lauren could see her reflection in the office glass behind him and there was shock and a stiffness she didn't recognize.

"Lauren, relax," he chided. "No one knows a thing and won't unless you give us away. Smile or something, will you?"

She tried, but a business smile of greeting was too hard to fake when all she could remember was her mouth fastened upon his swollen member. "God, but I miss you," she hissed under her breath while looking down at the coffee.

Justin smiled. "I know."

"What do we do now?"

"The same thing we've been doing all along, Lauren. The exact same thing."

"I don't think I can," she winced ever so slightly and a tear began to form in her eye.

"Sure you can, my girl. You're a pro, remember? Think of this as a courtroom and the people out there are the judges. Don't flinch and they'll lose interest. Remember, most of them work for you. It wouldn't be in their interest to gossip."

Lauren could feel her panties dampen as the words spilled from the mouth she had so recently kissed.

"Was he home?" Justin asked simply.

She shook her head. "I'm pretty sure he was still sleeping when I left," she added.

"Pretty sure?" he inquired, his eyebrows raised.

"We've had separate rooms for some time now," she explained.

Justin's heart leapt with this revelation; perhaps his quest wasn't so unreasonable after all. This was dangerous, he told himself. There was so much at stake. One wrong move and he could find himself separated from Lauren forever.

He looked at Lauren. "I don't know what to say," he began.

"Are you sorry?" she asked, surprised.

"Hell, no," he shot back. "I would do it a thousand times over if I had the chance."

She looked at him for long moments and then whispered, "Me, too."

At that moment, her secretary opened the office door and Lauren scrambled to cover the intimacy of the moment even though the energy was so charged with sexual attraction that Lauren thought surely everyone could feel it.

"Yes, Betsy?" Lauren said in an overly authoritative voice.

"Partners' luncheon at noon in the conference room," Betsy said crisply.

"Fine. Have my week's itinerary updated and to me at least fifteen minutes beforehand, please." Lauren looked at Justin for the length of a blink before continuing, "And Betsy," she added, "Justin will be working with me on the Bartley case. See that he has all the pertinent documents to review this afternoon and clear his commitments otherwise. For the time being, you will be serving as his support staff, as well as mine."

"Very well," Betsy nodded and looked briefly at Justin. She noted he did not look surprised, but seemed pleased somehow. He hadn't been in the office long enough for them to have a serious conversation. Perhaps they'd spoken by phone over the weather break. Regardless, she left to begin carrying out Lauren's instructions.

"I'm impressed," Justin said. "Think you can hold it together?"

Lauren looked up at him. "I don't have a choice. I need an excuse to explain why I get flustered when you're nearby. I need an excuse to explain why we spent the weekend together in case Aaron gets nosy. I need an excuse to be with you all day. And..." she added in a whisper, "I need an excuse for you to fuck me."

"Now?" Justin asked in a quirky tone. "Or would you like to save it for the partners' luncheon?"

"Get out," Lauren spat. "I have to get some work done and you're not helping matters. Get whatever you're working on wrapped up and begin with the Bartley case. Review the notes and tomorrow we'll start first thing going over the details and planning strategy."

"Yeeeees, sir!" Justin mocked and with a smile and salute, left her to her craving misery.

CHAPTER TEN

Lauren walked into the paneled conference room as its antique mantel clock sounded the twelfth hour. The room's three walls were lined with cherry shelving, laden with leather-bound law books dating back almost a hundred years. Anderson & Anderson was a firm that catered to old money, much of it from the equine industry that stretched over three states. The far wall held a fireplace crowned by an oil portrait of its founder, Mason Anderson, Sr., one hand tucked beneath the lapel of his tailored suit and the other holding his gold pocket watch; the style of his time. His eyes were shrewd and seemed to follow you as you moved about in this sacred room that held the secrets and confessions of clients in very high places.

Leather-covered straight, high-back chairs lined the massive cherry conference table. At every other seating sat an original, brass pen stand with inkwell. All business conducted in this room was signed with the same sort of tools used for a hundred years before;

you would find no computers in the boardroom of Anderson & Anderson.

The firm was now in the hands of Mason Anderson, Jr., himself a humped-over man well into his 70s. He had inherited the more unsavory traits of his well-connected father, including those connection friendships that are handed down from father to son. Mason, Jr. could, if called upon to do so, recite the bank balances of the state's wealthiest men, and even a few women; almost to the dollar. He made it his business to know anyone worth knowing and to distinguish anyone who was not.

Lauren had often wondered how it was she came to be invited to join this sanctum of inner sanctums, but she was not one to look a gift horse in the mouth. Perhaps they liked a pretty lady to look at as they decided the fates of the unfortunates; she had no quarrel with that as long as their power became hers as well.

The other partners were just filing in behind her, including her husband, Aaron. She looked at him briefly and his eyes were downcast but obviously sallow. She wondered what sort of debauchery had contributed to his look of illness and decided whatever it was, it didn't concern her. Just because both their ships sailed into the same port at night did not link them during the day; and she was all about sailing on her own.

Mason, Jr. was a widower and had been too angry to breed a son, or a daughter for that matter. Therefore every partner in the room was vying for that hallowed seat when the old lecher finally kicked off. Lauren was among them, although she knew the line was long and she was at the end.

She looked up at Aaron who was slouching in his regular seat opposite hers. He was watching her with those hollow eyes and she felt a moment of pity for him. Whatever his women were doing to him, he needed a break. Maybe she should suggest he take a vacation to some island in the sun. *Then I would be free to be with Justin in my own bed!* she thought to herself. Suddenly this became a wondrous idea and her mood rose visibly as Mason, Jr. called the meeting to order with his papery voice and teeth yellowed by age and a lifetime of pipe tobacco.

As Mason, Jr. droned on, occasionally asking for an opinion or report from one or the other, Lauren felt Aaron's eyes on her. Did he suspect something or was that guilt she was seeing? She looked up at him once and offered a smile; but he only nodded and then looked down at his section of the massive table.

The matter of the Bartley case was finally brought up and as Lauren solemnly answered the questions asked and brought everyone up to date, she felt a bit queasy as she added, "Justin will be working with me on this case. I think it's time he get some courtroom time and his background will be an asset." Mason, Jr. looked at her for a few moments, his heavy chin resting upon his chest nodding as he considered the positioning.

"Very well," he said after a moment and the other partners, with the exception of Aaron, nodded and muttered in obedient compliance. Aaron looked puzzled, as though trying to remember who Justin was but the look was quickly replaced by one of non-committal, as though he had more important things to consider. Lauren bit her tongue. *He doesn't give a shit what I do* she thought to herself. *That's okay, by the looks of him I'll be in that head chair long before he can get his ass out of whatever sling its in now.*

The meeting concluded shortly thereafter and as Lauren sailed from the room, she hesitated long enough next to Justin's desk to say, "Be here at eight. We need an early start," in a voice just loud enough to carry to Betsy. Indeed her secretary was already keying it in her calendar.

Lauren grabbed her handbag and left the office, not stopping to breathe until she was inside the Escalade and the heater was on full blast. "Monica?" she said, her cell in her hand and her best friend's voice at the other end.

"Hey girl, where are you?" came the spirited voice at the other end. "Did you fall off the map, or what?"

"I need some girl time. Can you meet me?" Lauren was already pulling out of the parking garage and headed down the busy street.

"Sure, I have nothing in the world to do," snapped Monica in mild aggravation. "Your wish is my command."

"Get off that throne, bitch," Lauren snarled. "Get Nikki if you can find her and meet me at Charlie's. I'll be there in a half hour."

"Anything you say, doll," came back the sarcastic voice. "Are you at least buyin'?"

"Just be there and you can eat the house and any man in it!" came Lauren's reply.

"Sounds like lunch, see you there," Monica's answer faded away as she was already hanging up.

Charlie's was a chic coffee shop that offered a full menu targeted to younger women of means. They opened at 11:00 a.m. and closed promptly at 5:00 p.m., just as the tea hour ended and the cocktails began. The wait staff had the signature look and behavior of young gay men who were always prepared with a ready quip and a bit of gossip to top off outrageously snarky compliments. The patrons loved this and flirted openly and safely, enjoying the ribald atmosphere and jokes. It was said if you were discussed at Charlie's, you'd made the grade. Straight men were discouraged from the hydrangea-flocked walls.

Lauren was checking the time on her phone just as Monica and Nikki approached the table. Cheek kisses were swapped and Monica and Nikki said little, seeing the storm ranging across Lauren's face. "You're late," she said in a catty tone.

Nikki was first to respond. "Well, bitch, if you're going to call in your ladies in waiting when this one is beneath Ricky Rouwega, you're just gonna have to cool your britches until I've cooled mine!"

Lauren rolled her eyes and Monica could not resist a snicker. "What are you laughing at?" Lauren glared at her.

"You!" Monica came back, setting her bag on the empty seat at the table. "What the hell got into you?" she asked and looked at Lauren's face. "Ohhhhweeee, let me rephrase that. *Who* the hell got into you?"

Lauren blanched. *Was it that obvious?*

"I'm sorry. You look delicious, both of you," she settled as the waiter came over and handed out menus.

"Ladies?" he said in a sing-song voice that was intended to suggest he was too busy to be nice for long and had better customers to see to.

The women ordered and tossed their menus back at him; a blatant dismissal that said *they* were too busy to worry about him.

"Alright, what the hell's up with you?" Nikki began.

"Aaron!" Lauren snapped, as if her husband were sitting at their very table. "He didn't drag his ass in until the wee hours and never once asked where I'd been all weekend!" She snapped the linen napkin off the table and settled it in her lap with anger.

Monica looked at Nikki. "Uh-huh....and just where *were* you all weekend?"

Lauren suddenly realized she'd set her own trap. It was time for a sidestep. "My car broke down in that horrid storm and I had to sleep in a strange bed for two nights, that's where! Aaron never asked a thing and when I finally got towed and home, he wasn't even there!"

"You're jumpin' to conclusions, Lauren," Monica said, gently placing her own napkin. "Aaron hasn't given you any reason to think he's bangin' someone, has he?"

"He looks like hell!" Lauren snapped, her mind rolling and fuming.

"Maybe he's just tired of working so damned hard. You said he wanted that chairman's chair, didn't you?" Monica fed back.

Lauren could feel dangerous waters beginning to rise about her. Time for a change of subject.

"Oh, never mind. I'm just out of sorts. Had very little sleep over the weekend and I'm starting on a new case, and it's not pretty," she fed them back. They seemed satisfied and Lauren relaxed a bit as Nikki began to relate the masculine qualities of her latest conquest.

Monica sat quietly, listening to Nikki but looking at Lauren repeatedly. She was no fool but it was obvious Lauren wasn't ready to spill the beans. *That's okay,* Monica thought to herself. *She's not fooling me but when she's ready to talk, she'll talk.*

CHAPTER ELEVEN

Nikki was on the phone. "Lauren, pleeeeeease come with me."

"Silly! It's only the dentist. You don't need an attorney just to go to the dentist." Lauren was checking her calendar as she spoke. "Anyway, I'm booked for court then."

"Lauren, I don't need an attorney, I need a friend. I absolutely hate the dentist and I just need you to hold my hand."

"Oh, for heaven's sake, Nikki. Look, I have an opening after three on Friday. Move your appointment and I'll drive you there."

"Got it—thanks, Lauren. You're a lifesaver."

Lauren nodded subtly as she clicked off the phone. *What I won't do for my girls,* she thought. She pushed open the door to the courthouse and found her way to the court clerk's office to file papers. *Someone should be doing this for me,* she thought. *Someone like Justin.* She had him deep in paper files and database research at the office; somehow asking him to run to the courthouse seemed like a waste of a good man. She was surprised at herself for being willing to take the back seat of importance in something as critical to her as her profession. *I'm losing it,* she thought. *I need to get a grip or I'll sail right out the door.*

The cell buzzed in her hand and in one smooth movement she answered. It was Monica.

"Hey, girl," came her voice, but it lacked its normal cheerfulness.

"What's up?" Lauren came back. "You sound down."

"You know…" Monica's voice trembled. "Another month, another disappointment."

Monica and her husband were trying to have a child. Although Monica seemed to be the more keen on the idea, Morgan appeared supportive, if somewhat distant.

"Hey, it'll happen," Lauren consoled. "You just have to relax and let Nature take its course. Have you considered seeing a doctor?"

"Have an appointment in a couple of weeks," Monica answered. "I hoped it wouldn't come to this, but it just ain't happenin' on its own. So, I'll go get tested and get some kind of diagrams or somethin'... Never thought I'd have to talk to a doctor to learn how to fuck!"

"It's not about fucking, Monica. It's about learning to be patient. You don't have a lot of that, you know." Lauren's voice was a bit motherly.

"Maybe...did Nikki get you?"

Suddenly Lauren realized she'd been railroaded. "Did she ask you first?"

Monica laughed, "Yeah, but I knew where she was headed as soon as she said the word "dentist" so I got off in a hurry. Told her I had to pee."

Lauren groaned, "Lucky you. I can't use that excuse in the car. Yes, she got me to go with her. Anything I should know?"

"Not as far as I know, but I'd bring some Handiwipes, though," Monica snickered.

"Handiwipes? What for?" Lauren asked.

"You'll find out," Monica sounded odd but the phone suddenly went silent and Lauren wasn't sure whether she'd disconnected or dropped a signal.

Lauren's thoughts were interrupted by yet another vibration on her phone. She looked down and saw it was a text...from Justin. She wheeled over to the shoulder and put the Escalade into park.

JUSTIN: WHERE ARE YOU?

LAUREN: HEADED BACK TO THE FIRM. WHY?

JUSTIN: WISH I WERE HEADED INTO YOU

...

JUSTIN: YOU THERE?

LAUREN: SORT OF

JUSTIN: MISSING YOU

LAUREN: FOR THE FIRST TIME IN MY LIFE, I'M WISHING FOR AN ICE STORM

JUSTIN: I KNOW HOW TO KEEP YOU THAWED

LAUREN: THIS IS MISERABLE

JUSTIN: I KNOW. WE'LL FIGURE SOMETHING OUT.

Lauren was so preoccupied as she drove back to the firm, that she missed her turn-off. Cursing under her breath, she was forced to drive another two miles to the next exit. It was an area populated by tall buildings whose offices catered to business professionals. She realized she would have to drive around the block to get back on the expressway and as she pulled up to the stop sign, she saw a very familiar shape entering the building on her right. She sat there, stunned. While she hadn't seen his face, she was sure her husband had just gone into those glass revolving doors. *Who's in there? We don't have any clients there.* Just then there was a horn behind her and Lauren pulled into the intersection and turned right. Sure enough, there was Aaron's car parked at a metered slot in the public parking.

Lauren debated her options. She could circle the block, park and head in to see where he might have gone. The building had twenty stories, though, and with her luck, he would walk into her elevator and then she'd have some explaining to do. And what if she found him? What would she do? Cause a scene? Hardly... not in public. Play innocent and attack him at home? She didn't want the confrontation; not because she was afraid, but because she didn't want to force a resolution. It was far easier to continue on the way they had been than to make up, or worse yet, separate.

Wiping a tear off her cheek, she completed the block and re-entered the expressway, heading back to their office. Time would tell.

"Nikki, for heaven's sake, stop whining," Lauren's patience was being tested.

"I haaaaaaaaate the dentist," Nikki's voice was nervous and she was obviously shaking. Lauren wondered at this woman beside her. Nikki was by nature brave and cocky, afraid of nothing.

"What's the matter with you? This isn't like you," Lauren observed, tugging Nikki's sleeve to enter the dentist's office building.

"Rotten teeth as a kid. Every time the old lady wanted to get back at me, she'd schedule an appointment. She knew it would hurt like hell and scare me into behaving. Problem was, she only let the dentist fix one tooth at a time, dragged it out. She wasn't going to lose her torture advantage."

"That's barbaric!" uttered Lauren.

"Yup. That's the old lady." Nikki was pale and sat in the waiting room chair. Lauren was forced to sign her in and when they were called, Lauren trailed her to the cubicle at the end. *Perhaps they know Nikki is a screamer,* Lauren thought. She'd been in the next room many times when Nikki was "entertaining" and knew Nikki had no sense of restraint.

Nikki climbed into the chair and settled back, arranging her skirt so that her legs looked to their advantage. The dentist, Dr. Wiseman, came into the cubicle shortly and settled down onto his little rolling stool. "Good morning, Nikki," he said with familiarity.

"Doc," she acknowledged. "Lauren, here, hold my hand," she begged, holding out a manicured display of fingers that rivaled fine art.

Dr. Wiseman picked through assorted stainless tools on the tray and then prodded Nikki's mouth open gently, tipping her head back so he could see. He poked around a bit and each time, Nikki howled. "I haven't started yet, Nikki," he said in a frustrated tone. Evidently this wasn't Nikki's first trip there.

Dr. Wiseman injected Novocain and tapped around a bit until it took effect. He finally seemed satisfied and pulled out the drill on its spring arm pivot. Lauren hated the sound of a drill herself, so she shivered somewhat as the whirring began. The drill began its preliminary heavy routering and Nikki's eyes opened wide. When the drill stopped, however, there was still a slight whirring sound and Nikki exhaled loudly.

Each time the drill stopped and just before it began, the distant buzzing sound repeated and each time Nikki's eyes opened and somewhat rolled upward. Dr. Wiseman noticed and cocked his head quizzically. "What's that noise?" he said in a curious tone, tapping the drill base as though looking for something loose.

Nikki's shoulders shrugged, as though she was somehow guilty but not wanting to admit it.

Wiseman said, "Huh," and picked up the drill. Once again the whirring began, although this time it didn't stop with the drill. His eyebrows went up but he continued his work. Evidently he'd decided to finish quickly before Nikki started screaming.

As for Nikki, she seemed surprisingly calm and content, even wriggling in the chair a bit as one does upon climbing beneath the covers on a cold night.

Finally Dr. Wiseman finished his work and left the cubicle to beckon to an assistant to finish up on Nikki and launch her out of the chair.

Soon, the assistant was done, the chair uprighted and Nikki was out of the door and into the daylight.

"Whew! I'm glad that's done," she said, practically skipping toward the car.

"That was strange," commented Lauren.

"What?" Nikki looked at her, eyes wide.

"There was that strange buzzing noise every time the drill started but when he was done, the noise stopped." Lauren opened the car and they climbed inside.

"Oh, that was me," Nikki commented as she buckled on her seatbelt.

"What do you mean that was you?" Lauren mused as she looked into the rearview to back up.

"My vibrator," Nikki's voice was casual.

Lauren stepped on the brakes at the exit of the parking lot. "What do you mean your vibrator?"

"My vibrator," Nikki repeated. "I've got one of those remote control babies loaded up and I use this little button to trigger it when that asshole starts his drilling," her hand opened to show a small, flat remote control with a flat black button and a tiny amplitude dial on its side edge.

"You what?" Lauren spurted out.

"Hey, you do what you gotta do to stay calm, right?" Nikki was matter of fact.

Lauren slammed the car into park and issued, "Ewwwwww...." as she scrambled for the tiny pack of Handiwipes she had brought in her purse, as instructed.

"Damn Monica," she cursed under her breath and Nikki just smiled and settled back. "Want to try it?"

Lauren handed Monica the Handiwipes. "Get that damn thing out of yourself. I don't want you leaking on my seats!"

"Jesus, you're uptight," Nikki responded, taking the package and reaching into the waistband of her skirt and panties. Her hand emerged and the egg-shaped device was wrapped loosely in the wipe. "Want me to put it in your purse so you can try it at the office? Or maybe in court?" Nikki teased.

"Get that away from me!" Lauren shrieked and considered dumping Nikki at the side of the road. Nikki just snickered and deposited the wrapped bundle into Lauren's expensive bag.

"Don't worry," she commented. "It's harmless without the remote."

CHAPTER TWELVE

"Lauren, do you have a moment?" came the rasping voice behind her as she was headed into her office. She didn't need to turn to know that Mason, Jr. himself stood planted behind her. He had the bulk of a man who took a few steps at a time and then stood his ground for a moment, as if adjusting to the dizzying momentum.

"Of course, Mr. Anderson," Lauren replied, handing her bag and case to Betsy and smoothly pivoting on one toe to follow him to his office set deeply at the window side of the office. Lauren could feel an unsettling come over her stomach, but this happened every time. She never knew whether she was to be raised on a dais or crushed on the carpet.

Mason indicated a chair with a nod and Lauren perched herself erectly on its leading edge. She held the stance of an alerted doe, ready to alight should danger be forthcoming.

"Lauren, it has come to my attention that you have taken Mr. Wilder under wing to help on the Bartley case," he began without prelude.

Lauren nodded. "He has some personal knowledge of the parties involved and therefore I thought he would prove helpful."

"I see. Why did you not opt for one of the other partners, say, perhaps, your own husband? Lauren, I won't mince words. The Bartley case is high profile and it's crucial we prevail. Anything less could be highly injurious to the firm. I need your word that you have this under control."

Lauren gulped. *How could this man touch upon so many sore spots all within a few sentences? That's why he's so good at his job. Witnesses don't have time to react before he spears them again and in confusion, they admit to everything without saying a word.* She had to admire his style and would be sorry to see him retire someday.

"Mr. Anderson, I feel I have the case well in hand, but if you feel otherwise, please include whomever you feel would be an enhancement. My strategy, so that you know, is to use fewer counsel at the table. If we appear we are defending en masse, so to speak, our client will appear all the more guilty. I want this to look like it's simply an afternoon's inconvenience."

"You're sharp, Lauren, sharper than I've given you credit for. Sexism aside, you're also attractive, young, ambitious, inquisitive and shrewd. Nothing against Aaron, I'm not sure what you saw in him, but that's neither here nor there." Anderson withdrew a cigar from a humidor on his desk, offering one to Lauren, who declined with a shake of her head. He was not the least bit intimidated with the no-smoking policy in the building. Mason Anderson, Jr. played by his own set of rules.

"It has been said, Lauren," he lit the cigar and tipped his chair backwards to enjoy the first puff, "that you have high aspirations."

"I do, sir, that's true." Lauren knew this was not a time to be coy.

His chair swung around to the side and he addressed her even though his gaze was on the crown molding of his paneled office wall. "And do these aspirations include Anderson & Anderson?"

Lauren hesitated for the briefest moment. Her answer could determine her own professional fate. "That, Mr. Anderson, would be up to you and the other partners."

Anderson chuckled, appreciating her candor. "Indeed it would, Lauren...indeed it would," he tapped ashes into a crystal tray on his desk. "Suppose you weren't slated for the head of the table?" he asked, referring to his own replacement. "What then?"

Lauren stood, angered by his condescending tone. How dare he compliment and support her one moment and then indicate that she was still left wanting! "I will sit at the head of a conference table, Mr. Anderson," she answered in an even, concentrated voice. "Yours or my own."

The rings of cigar smoke disappeared suddenly but Anderson maintained his composure; a quality he was well known for. His raspy voice, a product of corpulence and too many cigars returned the veiled threat. "Mutiny is punishable by death in most civilizations, Lauren. And if, by chance, the mutineer finds safe harbor where his captaincy is impotent, he has set an example for his own crew." The puffs resumed. "You do understand what I'm saying, don't you, *Ms. Reynolds*?" he emphasized her married name.

Lauren could not resist. "Aye," she said, turned and walked out of the office. She was shaking to her very core and tried to walk with composure back to her office. She retrieved her bag and went into the ladies' room. There she perched on a closed toilet, shaking and trying not to be sick. Finally she fished out her phone and texted.

LAUREN: I'M IN TROUBLE. NEED TO TALK.

JUSTIN: WHAT'S WRONG? WHERE ARE YOU?

LAUREN: MEET ME AT THE BAR IN THE HILTON AT 5:30, BACK BOOTH. BE SURE YOU AREN'T OBSERVED.

JUSTIN: ARE YOU OKAY? WHERE ARE YOU ANYWAY? I THOUGHT YOU WENT TO THE CAN.

LAUREN: I AM. JUST SITTING IN HERE UNTIL I CAN COME OUT WITHOUT CRYING. I'M LEAVING FOR THE AFTERNOON. SEE YOU AT THE HILTON.

JUSTIN: DARLIN' – I'LL BE THERE. LET ME KNOW IF YOU NEED ME IN THE MEANTIME. I KNOW A PLACE YOU CAN CHILL.

LAUREN: TOO DANGEROUS. JUST MEET ME.

JUSTIN: I'LL BE THERE.

Lauren composed herself, splashed cold water on her face and left the ladies' room. "Betsy, I have appointments of a personal nature this afternoon. Take messages and don't bother me unless it's critical. I will be in tomorrow morning," she said as she gathered a few documents and shoved them into her case in a show for those who were watching.

Her legs wobbling somewhat after the confrontation, Lauren steadied herself by grabbing a cup of water at the dispenser and again by stopping to admire a secretary's family picture while leaning against the desk. Finally she emerged into the sunlight and toward the Escalade. It had recently become her bastion of refuge.

CHAPTER THIRTEEN

Lauren's hands were shaking as she drove toward Monica's house. She needed some serious girl time right now and Monica was the only one who would take her seriously.

She used her key and opened Monica's front door to find her emerging from the bathroom, a narrow white object in her hand. Monica was crying.

Lauren threw her bag down on the side table and went to put her arm around Monica's shoulders. "I thought you already said this month was out," she said, indicating the pregnancy tester with the minus sign so blatantly stamped in red.

Monica's tears turned into a full-fledged sob and she flung the tester into the kitchen garbage. "I keep hoping the test is wrong," she whispered in a small voice between sobs.

"C'mon, sit down on the sofa and I'll make us some tea," soothed Lauren, headed toward the kitchen.

"Decaf," called Monica from the next room. "Caffine's not good for…" and new sobs could be heard. Lauren finished the tea preparation, added a few cookies and entered the living room with a tray to find Monica curled up on the sofa.

"Mon, c'mon, don't be like this. I can't stand to see you hurting," Lauren pleaded as she set the tray upon the coffee table. "You just need to be patient and to keep on trying, that's all. Some couples just take a little longer," she reminded her.

"Lauren, you just don't know what this feels like. I want to hold a baby in my arms and have it be my own. I sit here all day, alone, and there's no reason for my life." Lauren's eyebrows raised and Monica hurried on, "No, shit, I'm not knockin' myself off, so don't get all dramatic on me. I just want my life to stand for somethin', you know?" Monica looked at Lauren and then said, "Well, hell, you *don't* know, do you? Your life already does stand for somethin'. You've got the world by the ass, girl."

"If you only knew," Lauren muttered under her breath. She had come for girl time but knew this was no time to binge on bitching. Monica was hurting and it was time to help her, not add to her problems.

"Hey, look. Go wash that plain old face of yours and put on a dress. I'm taking you out for an afternoon of pampering and I won't take *no* for an answer." Monica was already shaking her head but Lauren pushed her up off the sofa. "Go ahead. I'm not leaving unless you're with me."

Monica sobbed a few more times, shuddering for breath between the way women do when they are truly crying from their soul. She nodded in agreement and disappeared up the stairs before returning fifteen minutes later, dressed and ready to go.

"There, that's better," said Lauren, heading to the front door. "Leave your purse. This afternoon is on me!"

The ladies headed for the most expensive department store in town and Lauren used her gold elevator key to access the floors normally closed to others. Sullivan's catered to several socio-groups, but none so thoroughly as those with bottomless credit cards.

When they stepped off the elevator they were greeted by a woman in a fitted black suit, her name inscribed as *Deliah* on the gold name badge. Deliah took them straight to a lounge decorated in salmon and gray. Long banquettes lined the walls and groupings of Queen Anne wingbacks faced mini raised dais. Lauren and Monica sat in one of these groupings and after Deliah ascertained what they were looking for, she snapped her fingers and a tray with champagne flutes and tiny sandwiches was brought out to them.

As they sipped, the models began to emerge from behind a curtained dressing room, each wearing an afternoon dress chosen to enhance first Lauren's, and then Monica's coloring and body shape. Lauren thought it would do Monica good to remember her womanly assets and certainly Lauren could stand a bit of feminine coddling as well. *If Anderson is going to treat me like a dimwitted peacock, then let him look at the feathers while I cut off his cock!* she thought to herself.

Since Lauren was driving, she stuck to one glass of champagne, but Monica was drinking it like lemonade on a hot day. Her posture had relaxed and she was smiling; something Lauren hadn't seen her do all day. She suspected there was more to the situation between Monica and Morgan but wasn't going to pry.

She reflected on her own situation and while she *ooohed* and *aaahhed* at the gowns being presented, she was checking her watch and waiting for 5:30 and her meeting with Justin. She had been inspired by anger, but was anticipating it with pure lust.

She and Monica each chose a dress and while they were being boxed and matched with shoes and a small bag, the ladies were whisked down the hall into private salons and treated to facials, manicures and pedicures. Lauren could feel the tension of the morning leaving her body and the craving for Justin grew stronger.

As they went back down to Lauren's Escalade, followed by a young man also dressed in stark black and carrying their purchases, Monica spoke up. "Lauren, that was a, a won..." she hiccupped slightly and had difficulty completing her sentence. The champagne was in control.

"You're welcome," Lauren finished for her. "Any time."

Lauren carried Monica's packages into the house for her and saw her to bed for a sleep-it-off nap. *At least she has quit crying* she thought.

Lauren just had time to run by the house and change her clothes before meeting Justin at the Hilton. To her amazement as she pulled into the drive, Aaron's car was waiting. She sat in her front seat for a few minutes to gather her composure. She hadn't counted on this.

Aaron met her at the door. "Darling!" he hugged Lauren and it felt weak. *Guilt takes a toll* she thought to herself as she returned his hug and handed him her packages to carry upstairs.

"Looks like my lady has hit the stores," he commented in a jocular manner. He seemed genuinely glad to see her. "I've missed you. How is it we're crossing paths? Let me take you to dinner," he invited, sincerely making an effort to be welcoming.

Lauren blanched. She hadn't planned on this. "Oh, Aaron, it's good to see you, too. I'm afraid I'm taking a late meeting this evening and not available for dinner. Can I take a rain check?" She held her breath.

He looked puzzled, but said nothing. "Of course, darling, whatever you say."

She looked into his compassionate brown eyes and wished she could confide in him about the Anderson interrogation earlier. *He would know what to do* she thought to herself. *But can I trust him? I know he has designs on Anderson's position as much as I do. Perhaps he's behaving just for now, waiting until he gets it and then he and his lady friend, or friends, will be off and my ass will be on the street.* It hurt to think of her own husband in this way, but there it was. Life was a series of moves and counter-moves and you could only trust your closest when there was a common enemy. Once that enemy was defeated, each was on their own.

Lauren followed Aaron upstairs and she gave him a hug and then playfully pushed him away as she went into her bedroom. "Have to grab a shower," she called over her shoulder. "Shopping is a dirty business, you know," she added laughingly. She turned on the spouts and began undressing when movements behind her made her catch her breath.

Aaron was standing in the bathroom doorway, watching her with hungry eyes. He had such a longing in them as he devoured her breasts and the triangle above her legs. She knew he wanted her, then and there. Wickedness forced her to smile, turn and step into the shower, picking up the soap to lather her breasts slowly, bubbles trailing over their rounded slopes and down her flat tummy. As the soap reached her fur, she parted her legs and using the liquid soap dispenser, slowly pumped a generous amount into her hands and then languidly slid her hand over herself, raising one foot to balance on the shower's seat.

The look in Aaron's eyes said it all. She could see him erect in his pants. As she turned to smile at him once again, he slowly turned, straightened his shoulders and quietly retreated, closing the door behind himself.

What is he waiting for? she wondered. Is it remorse for the other women? She felt a bit guilty for having put on such a display, but evidently he no longer wanted her. This hurt but at the same time gave her mental permission to meet, and be, with Justin. *Each to his own,* she thought to herself.

CHAPTER 14

Justin was waiting for her when she entered the bar at the Hilton. He stood and met her halfway across the room.

"Where have you been? I've been worried to death." His voice held angst and relief at the same time. "I want to kiss you so badly right now, you know," he added.

"I know. I'd like to be kissing you, too. And not just on your mouth," Lauren added.

"Let me get us a room," he pleaded.

"We could be seen," she answered. "The stakes have been raised."

"What do you mean?"

"Let's sit down and I'll tell you," Lauren fought the impulse to hug him and instead walked around him to establish a sense of business about the meeting.

Once they reached the table, she opened her case and began spreading papers around the surface.

Justin sat down across from her and pretended to be studying the papers as well. He said under his breath, "What's going on. Tell me."

"Anderson called me in," she began, looking up occasionally to see if anyone she knew was in the room.

"Okay...?" he said, waiting for her to go on.

"He brought up the Bartley case; said he wanted to make sure we had it under control."

"Do we? I mean, it appears open and shut to me, but maybe there's something you haven't told me?" he suggested.

"I scrambled. Told him I wanted just the two of us in court, minimize the importance of defense."

"Good cover, Lauren. You were born for this business."

"There's more."

"Go on..."

"Anderson threatened me."

Justin's posture stiffened and a dark look came over his handsome face. "In what way?"

"He suggested I might be looking to replace him and then more or less frosted that comment with an inquiry about what I would do if I weren't in the running."

"What did you tell him?" Justin's voice was grim.

"I told him the truth. That if I didn't replace him, I would leave."

"You told him that in so many words? Lauren, are you crazy?"

"He pissed me off! Flattered me and then shot me down as if I didn't amount to anything. What was I going to do? Submit and leave with my female tail between my legs?"

Justin sat back in the chair, spreading a well-muscled arm over the back. "Darlin', you've bitten off more than you know. You can't lose it like that. He doesn't play by the rules, and he has a whole nest of fellow vipers. You shouldn't be tweaking his fat nose."

Lauren was distraught. "I know, I know. I lost it. I've been kicking myself all day. I played my card before the hand was called. But it's too late now; he knows where I stand and that he and his cronies do not intimidate me. I don't know what he's liable to do, Justin. I don't think he'd risk scandal with Bartley as the client, but I'm not sure."

"He's in on it," Justin muttered. His brow was furrowed and she watched him loosen his tie.

"What? In on what?"

"Anderson." Justin leaned in closer so his voice could be heard. "You silly goose, Anderson was in on the fraud Bartley is accused of. He's a part of a very big network. He and every other man in the group take turns with the risk."

Lauren drew in her breath. "It goes deep, Lauren. No pattern, no accountability and they're all in it to cover each other's asses. Even the judge, for Christ's sake. He'll render the decision he's told and God help

117

anyone who appeals." Justin leaned back, shaken by the development. His Lauren was in serious danger.

"Are you saying I will be set up to lose?" Lauren whispered furiously. "Is that what the meeting was all about?"

"Of course, darlin'. He was picking your brain to see how much you knew. He leaves nothing to chance. You would have had the full support of the firm, of Anderson and all his cronies if you'd only answered something obliging. Now, there's no telling what they'll do. If he thinks you have a chance in hell of leaving the firm and making a name for yourself, he stands to be exposed and he'll not let that happen. He won't risk you taking him down because if he does...the others are next. Believe me when I say *they* won't let that happen."

Lauren began to shake.

"Darlin', get ahold of yourself. We'll figure something out." Lauren was shaking in earnest now and had big tears in her eyes. "Lauren! Stop it. Go to the can if you have to, but don't let anyone, not anyone, see you like this."

118

Lauren opened her handbag and tried to nonchalantly paw through the contents, as if looking for something. Finally, she snapped it shut and looked up at him. "What do I do?"

"Well, first of all, my darling Lauren, the word is *we*, not *I*. *We* have a few cards in our favor and the first is that Anderson doesn't think you have a clue what's going on. As far as he knows you're just an aggressive bitch with a heart of vengeance, pardon my language, darlin'." Justin was behaving casually to calm her down, but she knew him well enough to see the muscle jerking in his jaw and knew it meant he was pissed and worried.

"So," he went on, "let's not give him any reason to think differently. You just go on as normal. We'll do the research and build our defense. At the next partners' meeting you make a point of bringing up our strategy, suggesting that you're asking for the partners' permission to proceed. That will throw Anderson off and make points for you with the partners. You don't know who will succeed him, but you're going to need all the friends you can make." Justin relaxed a bit, feeling the adrenalin of an approaching battle fill his consciousness. He was a strategist. It was his calling.

"What about Aaron?" she asked quietly.

"What about him?" Justin's voice was tense. "For now, he's just another partner. Nothing more... nothing less. You said you thought he had something going on the side," Justin reminded her.

"I don't *know* that, Justin. I just know things have changed between us and we've become nothing more than what you see in the office," she finished.

Justin's muscle was jerking again. She knew that bringing up Aaron's name was probably a mistake, but the reality was, what it was, and they had to coordinate a plan or risk getting exposed. If that meant Justin was going to have to consider Aaron and her relationship, so be it.

"We have to win that case, Lauren. You know that, don't you?" Justin's voice was tense.

"I know. I *always* go in to win."

"This is different. You won't have any idea which way the judge is leaning before you even walk into the courtroom. We need to prove, beyond a doubt to the jury that Bartley is innocent. We can't give that power of persuasion over to the judge, in case he's been instructed otherwise."

"Why would they risk Bartley?" she asked, perplexed.

"The sacrificial goat, darlin'. These boys all know what they're risking when they jump in. Sometimes, one of them has to take a hit, but as long as it's *all between friends* so to speak, the victim will get his share and all will be made right. Lauren, if they believe for one minute that the fire is out of their control and that you're holding the fire hose, all bets are off. I'm serious. Do you understand?"

Lauren nodded, feeling small and raw again, like the star struck girl from Texas with big dreams. She was out of her league and she knew it. She needed Justin more than anything right now. She looked up to his eyes.

"Stay the course, Lauren. Just stay the course," he urged, a tinge of frantic in his voice. "I've got your back and we're not without friends of our own, believe me. But you have the front seat on this. There's only so much I can do. Stay the course," he repeated and risked patting the back of her hand in the darkness of the corner table.

"I want you," she said simply.

"No more than I want you right now, darlin'" He looked over his shoulder. "Let me get us a room. I'll go up first and text you the number. You can follow when you think the time is right."

"I can't. Aaron thinks I'm in a business meeting and will be expecting me. He's already feeling...ignored."

"I don't get you, Lauren," his voice was angry. "You know he's screwing around and yet you play the role of obedient wife. Where the hell do *we* get a part to play?"

"I don't know for sure what he's doing, or which side he's on, Justin. I can't take that chance and you

122

know it. You just told me to stay the course…well, my course is that I'm still married to Aaron and for now, as long as he's tracking me, that's the way I'm going to behave. If this thing is as deep as you say, we have to put survival first and play second." Lauren was equally angry, but not at Justin. She was angry that she had let herself be placed in this position; that she had given away her power. She felt like a puppet and it didn't sit well.

"You're right, I know. I just want you so badly right now, Lauren."

"Me, too. Go now, Justin, before I give in. Please," she pleaded quietly.

Justin nodded, downed the rest of his drink and slammed the glass down on the table a little harder than necessary. "See you tomorrow," he said and left.

She watched him go and felt as though she knew what the passengers on the Titanic had felt as they watched the last lifeboats rowing to escape the great sucking pressure that would take the ship to its grave.

Lauren let herself in the front door and slipped off her heels. Aaron was sleeping in the recliner in front of the television. As she went to pick her handbag off the side table in the foyer, she saw his briefcase and iPhone abandoned there.

She picked up the iPhone and quickly did a check of his contacts. She knew his password. Aaron, if anything, was predictable. He always used the date of their wedding followed by her first name. She didn't spot anything there that looked out of place. She looked through his apps and checked a few other things, then carefully placed it back where it originally sat. One last check at Aaron to see he was still snoring quietly and she went upstairs, alone. *Somebody's going to pay* she swore to herself.

CHAPTER FIFTEEN

Nikki bounced down the stairs to the dank little club hovering below the street level. It was one of her favorite places to go when she was *in the mood.*

It took a few minutes for her eyes to acclimate to the darkness; this was the sort of place where you came to do serious drinking or to buy your powder recreation for the evening. People came here to forget the others they met; there was very little desire for illumination.

"Nikki!" came several voices, anxious for her to alight next to them. They knew when Nikki was in the mood; it was written all over her face.

She took a minute to survey the room and take roll call. She laughed as one of her regular friends was crouching low; his wife at his table. "How ya doin' Scotty boy?" she ruffled his hair as she passed him. The wife frowned and kicked him, filling Nikki with delight.

125

She enjoyed her power over men. It had less to do with beauty and more to do with her carefree attitude. She exuded self-confident charm and men found this irresistible.

Nikki was wearing a preppy little cheerleader skirt with a tight white, v-necked sweater. She had a tattoo of an elaborate Victorian arrow at the top of her cleavage and pointing downward. Those lucky enough to go home with her would find another matching arrow below her navel.

She finally settled on an empty stool at the bar's end; this gave her better vantage and happened to be right next to the men's john so eventually, every single one of them passed right by her perfume. She never even bothered to bring a purse; there was a never-ending supply of drinks purchased on her behalf.

On this evening, the door opened and someone new to the crowd stepped inside. Nikki could see by his silhouette that he was very tall; God, but she loved tall men. At 5'10" herself, she loved the feeling of male flesh lying atop her and extending beyond her feet.

The silhouette moved closer and surprisingly took a stool next to her. "Is this seat taken?" came the familiar phrase.

"Depends on why you're here," she responded, licking her lips.

He turned to look at her and Nikki could see gleaming white teeth, even in this darkness. "Do I pass muster?" he asked, smiling.

Nikki twirled the tiny umbrella in her drink and coyly said, "That remains to be seen, but you can sit there for the time being."

"I'm Brad," he said, holding out his hand.

"I'd ask you if that's short for Bradley, but from what I can see, you're not short on anything," she purred, letting her eyes wander down his length suggestively.

"You're quite a little minx, aren't you?" he said, waving the bartender to give him the same thing Nikki was drinking and ordering another for her at the same time.

"I would rather pet it than be it," she shot back.

Brad leaned backward as if shot. "Wow, you certainly don't waste time. Are you...professional?" he asked hesitantly.

Nikki gurgled a laugh, "If you mean do I charge, no, don't need the money. If you mean do I know what I'm doing, I'd say you could be the best judge of that."

"You are incorrigible," he laughed. "I don't think I caught your name?"

"I'm Nikki," she said, holding out her hand and when he took it she pulled his up to her lips, kissed his middle finger and then pushed it under her skirt. Brad's response was to run it up the inside of her thigh until it found its target. He flicked her and Nikki felt the rush of blood and heat she had come looking for.

"You know," she said, climbing off the stool and pushing her half-full drink toward the bartender, "I believe I've had enough to drink. Think I'll head home and see what sort of trouble I can get into. Interested?" she finished and looked at Brad with a twinkle in her eye.

"Couldn't drink another sip," he commented, pushing his drink forward and throwing a twenty on the bar. "After you," he said, bowing and stepping back to let her pass.

Lauren was in the law library, piles of books surrounding her. Justin was seated across the table from her and between them they were planning strategy. She was dictating and he was taking notes. No one could see her stockinged toe massaging his crotch, but it made it difficult for him to work.

"I wish you would do that when we're alone," he commented, distracted.

"It wouldn't be as much fun," she smiled and bent back to her books. "We need to find something that everyone has forgotten; some obscure defense that no one has tried in forever. There has to be something here."

"Lauren, if it's here, I will find it. Why don't you go home and get some sleep. You've been here for sixteen hours already and you need your beauty sleep, darlin'."

"In a minute. I'm sure it's here…" she continued, running her finger down the page.

Justin shut the book gently on her hand. "Lauren, I've got this. Go home. Eat. Shower. Sleep. Got it?"

Lauren wondered why his words didn't inflame her sense of dominion. She knew why…he was right.

"Okay, I give," she said. "I'll see you in the morning, Justin."

She stood and stretched, her breasts expanding the fabric of her blouse. "Any more of that and I'll be going with you," Justin observed. He laughed gently, "Really, I've got this. Go. I'll text you if I find anything."

Lauren nodded and headed out the door. Aaron was standing in the doorway of his office, watching her. She smiled at him but wondered if knew anything. He looked so hollow around the eyes. *It's not my problem any more,* she thought to herself and grabbing her bag, left the office and went home.

CHAPTER SIXTEEN

Lauren walked in the front door and Aaron was waiting for her. She hung her coat in the hall closet, slipped off her shoes and picked up her bag to go upstairs. She had no appetite for anything, but sleep.

"Lauren?" came Aaron's voice. "Darling, come in here, please. I'd like to spend a few minutes with you before you go off to bed."

Lauren kept her sigh to herself, but if *staying the course* meant maintaining some semblance of normalcy in her home life, so be it. She walked into the living room and plopped down in an oversized wingback chair upholstered in muted paisley. Her stockinged feet slid onto the ottoman and she blinked to keep her eyes alert.

"Hi," she said in a friendly, if exhausted voice.

"Hello," Aaron answered, tapping his pipe on the ashtray at his side. His eyes looked hollow and the skin on his face hung from his cheeks.

Jesus, he looks bad, thought Lauren. "How have you been? Seems like forever since we've talked," she said.

"It has been forever," he answered. "You've been making yourself pretty scarce." Aaron didn't seem resentful; he had more of a thoughtful tone of voice.

Lauren laid her head back against the chair and looked around the room. It was warmly decorated with muted colors. While she had hired a decorator, she had supervised the color palette and fabric selections. There was a fireplace built into one wall with a flat screen hanging above it. She had begun to collect art and a few pieces that were rather collectible already graced the walls.

"Are you hunkered down on the Bartley case?" Aaron asked.

"Of course," she answered, perhaps a bit shortly. *Is he watching me for them?* she wondered.

"The firm is very interested in that case, you know, darling," he said. "Do you need help?"

"No, I've got it," she replied. "Justin is combing the library as we speak," she added, closing her eyes.

"You and Justin seemed to have hit it off," he commented, tapping his pipe again. "How did you happen to choose him?"

Lauren kept her eyes closed, as much to buy time to come up with a response as to appear nonchalant. "He's smart, connected, ambitious and unlike some of the partners, not insecure because I'm a woman," she replied.

Aaron seemed thoughtful at this, unsure how to discuss it. He knew Lauren was a proud woman, had accomplished more than most women her age and had her reputation to think about. "Darling, even the best attorneys need to reach out, you know. Being a woman has nothing to do with it. You're highly respected."

"Perhaps," she granted, "but not by the men who sit at the table with me every day. I seem to be a token; a pet darling they're planning great things for." She opened her eyes and sat forward in the chair, looking directly at him. "I'm nobody's pet, Aaron. Least of all the firm's," she said smoothly, standing to go upstairs.

Aaron flipped off the table lamp next to him and laid down the pipe. He followed her up the stairs. "Would you sleep with me tonight, darling?" he asked in a somewhat plaintive tone.

"Not tonight, Aaron. I'm exhausted and need my strength." She felt bad to shut him down this way. "Maybe when the trial is over," she added as an afterthought. That would buy her some time at least.

She went into her bedroom and shut the door behind her. As she sat on the edge of her bed, she peeled off her stockings, removed her blouse and skirt and sat there for some time in only her slip and panties. She felt exhausted, not only for the long hours but the constant anxiety of being watched and planning her own protection. *Who can I truly trust? Who doesn't have some sort of stake in this? No one, at least no one who can do me any good.*

At some point Lauren simply turned sideways, shut off the light on the nightstand and slid beneath the covers, not even bothering to undress further. She closed her eyes and went to sleep.

Monica padded downstairs in her stockinged feet, searching for a cup of coffee. The Keurig was primed and she simply inserted her decaf favorite and hit the button. Morgan was at the kitchen table, the Saturday paper in his hands. He seemed preoccupied with the sports section and she popped bread into the toaster before saying anything.

"Did you sleep well?" she asked him.

"Hmmm...yeah," he answered without looking up.

Monica looked out the curtained window while waiting for the toast. Her kitchen was pristine white with vivid red accents. She liked the color red; it was warm and yet made her personal statement. The toast finally popped up and she carried it with her coffee to the table.

"Morgan?" she began.

"Yeah?" he barely looked up from his paper.

"Honey, you know how badly I want a baby," she said.

"Yeah, I know," he still did not look up.

She wasn't sure how to say the next part, but had been screwing up her courage to do so over the past week. "Morgan, would you go and get tested?" she asked bluntly.

"Tested?" he still studied the paper.

"You know, honey...to make sure your boys can get to my girls," she tried to put it in the least clinical terms possible.

"Don't need to," he said, flipping the page to the business section. "The boys are fine."

Monica felt ignored and as if she was in the marriage alone. She knew Morgan wasn't as crazy about having a baby as she, and yet he had agreed and so should at least give her the support and participation they had agreed upon.

"You don't know that for sure," she tried to appeal to his sense of nurturing. "I've been to my doctor and they said it should be happening."

"I said the boys are fine, Monica. What more do you want from me?" Morgan was looking up from his paper now and the expression on his face did not bear arguing with. As far as he was concerned, the subject was closed. He got up and left the table. Soon after she heard him go out the front door, closing it none too gently.

Monica's tears dripped into her coffee. She didn't understand Morgan's attitude and it made her feel so alone, so abandoned. She was feeling overwhelmed; not only was she depressed because she wasn't getting pregnant; she felt like she was losing her husband at the same time.

She resolutely stood up, rinsed the dirty dishes before putting them in the dishwasher and then went upstairs to shower. After dressing, she walked down the hall to the third bedroom they used now as an office. It would be the nursery, *if I ever get to use it* she thought to herself. She sat in the office chair there and used her imagination to picture a crib with a wriggling newborn. She imagined how she would decorate it and wondered whether she'd want to know ahead of time whether it was a boy, or girl. She pictured mint green with stuffed monkeys and maybe a giraffe. Or perhaps it would be a girl and she could build and furnish the doll's house she'd dreamed of having as a child herself.

Would Morgan make a good father? Would he be loving and supportive; take his turn at changing diapers? Or would he be sulking and disassociated, as he was this morning when she tried to talk about it with him?

She had the impulse to begin cleaning the room. Perhaps if she prepared the nursery it would trigger all the right magic to create a new life. *But,* she thought to herself, *if it still doesn't happen, seeing a nursery would be too much; I couldn't bear it.* With that she left the room, closing the door softly behind her so as not to disturb whatever baby energy there might be left behind.

CHAPTER SEVENTEEN

Nikki opened the door to the knock and found Brad standing in her doorway. Her thick, red hair tousled; she had been still sleeping and was confused.

"Hi?" she tentatively offered. "Did I miss something?"

"Hi, yourself," he said, pushing past her, his arms filled with bags of groceries. "Glad to see you're getting some rest. I've brought breakfast," he said cheerily, setting the bags on the counter and beginning to pull things out. "Do you have a medium-sized frying pan?" His voice was casual, but his attitude was decidedly in control.

"Uhhh, I suppose so," Nikki faltered, trying to figure out what was going on. *I'm slipping. Was he here last night?*

Brad was a bit psychic. "No, I wasn't here last night. It was three nights ago and you were pretty loaded so I'm not sure if you remember at all. Doesn't matter, I'm here now." He found the pan and tapped in a healthy lump of butter. "You like omelets, right?"

"Why?" Nikki asked.

"Because that's what I'm making. A fresh spinach and ham omelet, topped by white cheddar." He looked at her, "You are hungry, right? Well, you do look a bit pale...have another late night?"

"No, I mean why are you here?" Nikki said again to clarify.

He stopped and looked at her squarely. "Because, my sweet Nikki, someone has to look after you. You're not doing a very good job and I've decided I'd like to give it a try."

Nikki was speechless. She seldom remembered the names of the men she brought home. She was more focused on other parts of their anatomy. She had *never* had one return; much less on his own!

Brad was whisking eggs while the ham and spinach bits sizzled in the butter. "Want to make some coffee?" he suggested.

Nikki shrugged and flipped on the Keurig. At least *that* she could handle.

"Do you want to set the table?" Brad suggested, his back to her as he stood at the stove.

Nikki was a bit flabbergasted at his impudence, but in a way, it was completely enticing and sexy. She was used to "being on top" and this gorgeous specimen of a man had not only "topped" her the other night, but was now ordering her around...and she liked it.

She quickly laid place settings and then disappeared into the bedroom to pull on a pair of jeans and a t-shirt, omitting any underwear, just in case. When she returned, he had placed her cup of coffee on the table alongside a plate with the most appetizing omelet she'd ever seen. *Maybe because I don't ever cook* she thought. She took the seat and he soon joined her.

"So, to what do I owe this unexpected pleasure?" she began in her normally cocky style.

"I like you," he said simply, "as a matter of fact quite a bit. But you're rough around the edges with

141

neglect. I can't stand to see a perfectly good woman be less than her best; simply because she needs to be loved. So, here I am, up to the job and applying with your permission," he finished, a laconic smile dancing across his handsome face.

Nikki looked at him, trying to decide whether he was serious and figuring she had nothing to lose, she answered, "You're hired." She smiled and added, "So...I know you can cook," she pointed to her plate, "and I know you can fuck," she pointed to her crotch. "What else are you good at?" Her eyes dared him to match her.

"You don't remember?" he asked, mocking her. To his pleasure, she did look momentarily confused.

"Well... I thought I covered that," she said, pointing again to her crotch.

"Then you weren't paying attention," he returned, forking a large bite into his mouth. "I guess I'll have to remind you," he added.

Nikki smiled, and was glad she'd left off her underwear.

142

Smoke billowed lazily toward the coffered ceiling as Mason Anderson sat back in his chair, his feet crossed on a short footstool no one knew he kept beneath his desk. The heavier he'd become, the more back pain he suffered. His doctor had suggested raising his feet to take strain off the back, as well as relieve some of the swelling in his feet. Anderson was not a well man, but he was content with that. He had no children, no reason to live long and so he traded self-indulgence now for years of abstinence and a bedpan later. In his opinion, it was a fair deal.

He was on the phone, his rasping voice muted in secretive conversation.

"She's on it, the bitch," he muttered. "Got that greenhorn Wilder lapping at her cunt; nothing to worry about there." He paused as the voice at the other end make comments. "I don't give a hot damned what Bartley wants! He's going down, and taking her with him. She is a risk that must be dealt with," he said in measured words, underlining their importance.

The voice said something more; something that insulted his capabilities. "Listen carefully," he growled. "We're doing this my way and I'll brook no interference. The fix is in and we knew that eventually, one of us would take it; it was inevitable. She was more than I bargained on, the damned bitch. Bartley will just have to eat dick for a couple of months and then he will be compensated appropriately. I have this taken care of. This is the last I will speak of it," and with that, he hung up the phone.

He sat for some time, watching the smoke curls and plotting the details. At one point, he chuckled to himself. How he loved the game; it's what kept him alive.

At one point, he heaved to his feet, picked up his briefcase and ambled slowly out of the office in search of Baked Alaska, a bottle of his favorite Bordeaux and the all-too-willing mouth of Rodney, his latest subordinate. Life was good, but nailing bitches was better.

CHAPTER EIGHTEEN

Lauren walked into the office on Monday morning and even before she laid down her bag, Justin was at her doorway, an anxious look on his face.

She nodded him to come in and he closed the door behind himself. "What is it? You look upset."

Justin sat down in the chair opposite her desk, leaning backward as if in nonchalance, although his voice was anything but. "I need to discuss the Bartley case with you."

Lauren looked up from tossing a note into the wastebasket and saw his face held true concern. A lock of her hair had fallen over her forehead and the effect was endearing.

Justin drew in his breath just looking at her. He wanted her so badly he could feel himself hardening and wanted to throw her across the desk and take her then and there. He tried to focus.

145

"There are some facts I've discovered that warrant your attention," he said, his words measured as one does when they're trying to communicate an entirely different message.

She nodded in understanding and tried to lean back in her chair and even smile a bit.

"I wonder if you have a block of time this morning? What I need to show you is not in the office."

She responded, "Of course, I believe my calendar is open all morning. Would you care to go now?"

Justin stood, signifying that's exactly what he wanted and he followed her, a careful three paces behind, as they exited the building.

"My car or yours?" she asked.

"Mine will be fine." They walked to the outer ring of the parking garage where everyone but partners parked and climbed inside. Justin started the car and they soon pulled out into traffic.

146

"Okay, what's this all about?" she asked as soon as they were cruising.

"I want you to stay calm, do you promise?" he asked first, patting her hand. She nodded. "I mean it, Lauren. Don't get scared, and whatever you do, don't get pissed. It will be easy to spot and that could make matters much worse."

"Okay, okay, I promise. Now what's up?" Her dark eyes were filled with concern and he wanted to kiss her and tell her it would be okay, but that was something he could not promise.

"You're being followed." His statement was short and abrupt.

"What? How do you know?" her voice became steely hard.

"Because I followed you and there was a black sedan between us the entire time." He stopped here, letting her absorb it.

"Why were you following me?" she asked, a bit angry.

"For precisely the reason I just explained. I need to know what they know and how close they are to you." His eyes were on the road but he shot sideline glances at her to see how she was reacting. "There's more. Your phone is bugged, your email is being monitored and someone has been tampering with our computer records on the Bartley case."

"What do you mean, tampering?"

"Documents have dates changed, amount of money, small details you wouldn't notice if you'd already studied everything. Most everything has already been filed as evidence so it would simply confuse you in court...make you look ill-prepared and damage your credibility."

"And you know this...how?" she asked.

"It's what I do, Lauren. I told you I had your back. I'm not a total fucking idiot, you know, darlin'."

"Of course not. I didn't mean..." Lauren was at a loss. This information had a huge impact on how she was going to get through this undamaged. "Who...?"

Justin rolled his eyes and that said it all.

"Why don't they just take me off the case?" she asked, perplexed. "Send me on vacation...put one of the other partners in charge?"

"Because, my dear Lauren, Bartley is expendable, at least in the immediate future. You, on the other hand, are not. You pose a risk because you're smart and they can't get rid of you because you're smart enough to double back and catch them at their own game."

"Smart enough, only if I have you on my side," she commented, shivering at the thought of possibilities.

"We're a team, darlin'," he said, "or did you forget?"

"Of course not. I'm just not used to the idea. I've always gone it alone." She couldn't help it but her eyes misted.

"Those days are over, darlin'," he patted her hand again.

"The problem is, I don't know how deep this goes," she mused. "Any ideas there?"

"I don't think it really matters, Lauren. You take the head off the snake and the rest is useless. At the same time, if you focus on the rattle, the head will bite and you're done."

"So, what do I do?" She felt helpless, depending on Justin for answers. She was supposed to be a professional; to be resourceful and have the command of the law within her hands. She was not used to being the victim.

"For now, nothing. It's enough that you know what's going on and don't leave anything for them to find. I expected this and had already backed up the documents before they got to them. You won't go into court with anything that isn't verified a hundred times by me, personally." Justin's manner seemed to calm her a bit, or so he hoped. She was the captain of this ship and if she faltered, there was no one but him to catch her and he didn't have the credentials. It was very important that she not become overwhelmed.

"Where are we going?" Lauren asked as the city landscape gave way to the country.

"We're driving out of town so the traffic is sparse and we can spot whomever is tailing us easier. When he gives up, we'll go to my place. I want to make love to you."

Lauren looked at him with a bit of shock. "You don't waste words, do you?"

"Not with a lawyer, I don't. I tell it like it is," he smiled and kept looking into the rear view mirror. As side roads came up, Justin selected a variety of them, sometimes ending up back on the same main road. Eventually he seemed content they were alone and he headed for his house.

Inside, Justin wasted no time. He scooped Lauren up in his arms and carried her into the bedroom. He deposited her on the bed, still standing. While she watched, he removed his suit, letting it pool on the floor behind him. He unbuttoned his shirt, revealing the planes of his chest with excruciating slowness. When each button lay to the side, instead of slipping out of the shirt, his thumbs went into the waistband of his shorts and he began to lower them.

Lauren cried out in protest, falling against his arms to arrest their progression. She pulled him toward her but did not permit him on the bed. She took his arms and positioned them as one would a clay model, palms outward and bent at the elbow as though in surrender. He moved to reach for her, but she slapped him hard and put his hands back into the air. She could see the muscle jerking in his cheek; he was not a man accustomed to surrender.

She stood on the bed and removed her own suit, kicking off her shoes and sliding off the pantyhose. Now she slowly unbuttoned her own blouse, each button release causing the cloth to gape and reveal that she wore no bra beneath. Justin's eyebrows rose at this, but he said nothing.

Finally Lauren stood clothed exactly as he, the difference in their height made equal by her standing on the bed. She came close now and kissed him on the hollow at the base of his throat. Then she took his hands and placed them at the collar of his shirt, doing the same with hers. She moved forward once again, this time opening her blouse and letting her soft flesh nestle against his chest, revealed by his hands as well.

In sync, they slid off their shirts and now stood skin to skin, her nipples hard and erect, as was his penis. Hands could hold back no longer and he reached to cup her breasts while she ran hers across the hairs of his chest and feather-touched his nipples. Their breathing came faster and she began to moan with each stroke of his hand upon her. As if in agreement, both let their hands travel to the last article of clothing and lowered it upon one another. When Lauren kicked her panties free onto the floor, Justin took his hand and parted her legs, cupping her fur and inserting his finger into her. Lauren took his penis in her hands, sliding the skin tight and upward and then cupping his balls with one hand. She groaned at the sensation he was creating in her and her legs finally buckled and she collapsed upon the bed. He lay next to her and they fed upon one another, each trying to give pleasure but unable to ignore their own needs.

Lauren felt the hot lava deep in her pussy beginning to erupt and her breathing changed. Justin knew this instinctively and swung around to dive into her deeply with his massive erection. He placed his hands beneath her bottom and drove so deeply that he could feel his own impact within her. She screamed with the guttural cry of a woman who was completely possessed by her man; an instinct that left her unaware of anything or anyone but him.

Justin pulled out slowly, almost to the point of exit before driving in hard again. Lauren responded, her hips lifting to keep him from escaping, the walls of her vagina clamping down upon him like a velvet trap.

"Give it to me, Lauren," he bit the words out in a hard whisper, commanding her to surrender. "I want to feel you burst, just as I burst and then I will kiss you clean. C'mon, darlin', give it to me. I need you so badly. You belong to me, no one else, and I'm claiming it right now and right here. Lauren, give it to me!"

She burst then, great waves of sensation so intense she thought she would pass out. Lightning shafts illuminated her brain, even with her eyes closed and for a time, she felt consumed with a pleasure she had never imagined. Justin exploded within her at the same time and the heat seared them equally. The scent of raw sex filled the air about them, each of them straining to remember the sensations and smells of this moment.

It was a moment that eclipsed anything either of them had ever known.

CHAPTER NINETEEN

Lauren's cell rang and Monica's voice was clearly hysterical. "I need you now!" came her strangled words.

"What's wrong, Mon?" Lauren was overwhelmed with paperwork and not really in the mood for girl talk but there was something very compelling about Monica's voice.

"Just come!" Monica sounded unlike herself. Lauren couldn't ignore it, no matter how inconvenient the timing.

"I'm on my way shortly," Lauren reassured her. The response was a dead line. Lauren was very concerned but she had a filing deadline she could not afford to miss.

"Hello?" Nikki's sleepy voice came on the line.

"Nik, something's wrong with Monica," her statement was to the point.

156

"What?"

"I don't know. She just called me, hysterical, and insists I come right over. I absolutely cannot leave for at least an hour. Can you go over?"

"Sure, let me get dressed," Nikki answered and Lauren wondered why Nikki wasn't dressed when it was well after noon. Then she heard a deep male voice in the background, questioning where she was going and that answered it. Nikki's voice was muffled as she made a comment to the male voice and then she was back on the line. "I'll leave in ten," she reassured Lauren. "You come when you can but don't worry— I've got this."

"See you then," Lauren's finger was already on the *End Call* button, halfway down to her desk.

She motioned to Justin through the glass of her office. He came in with a quizzical look on his face. Like her, he was deep into research for the Bartley case.

"What's up? You look worried," he commented.

157

"It's Monica. Something is wrong and she's begging me to come over. We both know I can't go until these papers get filed. I've got Nikki headed over but this is my best friend; I can't leave her alone too long. She's...well...a little unstable right now. Long story. Can you help?"

"Of course, what do you need?" Lauren motioned him around the desk and indicated the papers before her.

"These need to get completed and then the info put into the system. We'll file electronically before anyone has a chance to make these disappear."

"Good idea," he said. "I've got it. You go on."

"No, I have to sign them and I'm not taking the chance of having you do it for me and us getting caught. This is both our asses on the line."

"I like your ass, let's get it off the line," he teased, trying to lighten the moment.

She smiled and winked. "If you'll get the data for these," she handed him a stack, "and put it into the system, I'll take care of the rest. That will cut my time in half," she looked up at him.

"Say no more, darlin'," he answered and was on his way out of the door.

At that moment her secretary came in and stood aside to let him pass. She looked at Lauren and could tell she'd walked in on something more than business, but said nothing. She liked her job.

"Mr. Anderson would like to see you in his office immediately," she informed.

"Fuck!" Lauren swore. "I don't need his shit now."

"Sorry, but his secretary was quite insistent. Anything I can do?" Betsy asked.

"No, wish you could. Let me see what Anderson wants and then I'll be back. Hold all my other calls, no exceptions." She checked her hair in a hand-held compact and dusted her nose before grabbing a pen and steno pad and heading toward Anderson's office.

Inside she found Mason, his bulk obscuring the window inside, she shuddered. "Close the door, please," he ordered in a not so polite tone.

Lauren obliged and then went to take a chair, surprised to see her husband sitting in the other. *What is this? A fucking marriage counseling?* she thought to herself.

"Lauren," Anderson began, "I've called you here to discuss the Bartley case. I'm not very pleased with what I'm seeing." His voice was curt and to the point.

"Oh?" she asked and it took everything she had not to turn and look to Aaron for support. It would have undermined her authority in the room, permanently.

"Wilder isn't enough," Anderson continued. "You need more experience to back you up, even if it's not in the courtroom. I want Aaron to come on board," he said in a voice that spelled finality.

Lauren quickly checked the clock on Anderson's desk. She didn't have time for this shit and knew it would be pointless to argue anyway.

"Okay," she capitulated. "Whatever you say."

160

Anderson looked at her. He seemed a bit taken aback at the readiness with which she agreed. His corpulent face flushed with indecision. *What kind of game is this bitch playing? I expected more kick out of her.*

Lauren looked at him expectantly. She still didn't risk a sidelong look at Aaron. That would reveal how little they communicated and there was no way she wanted Anderson to sense this.

Anderson studied her and then looked at Aaron, "You on board, Aaron?" he asked, tipping ashes from his cigar into the crystal tray on the corner of his desk.

Lauren had no choice now but to look at Aaron. She noticed once again how dark his eyelids looked. Inside she felt disgust with whatever lifestyle he was leading that would encourage him to let himself go like this. It made her look bad, as well. Aaron swallowed hard and spoke up, "Of course. I'll have Lauren bring me up to speed and you can rest easy, Mason." He looked at Lauren for approval and she nodded slightly. They both looked up at Anderson to gauge his response.

161

What the fuck are these two up to? Anderson thought to himself. He knew all was not well in the Reynolds household but he didn't give a fuck unless it served his purpose. *Let the bitch stew a bit* he thought to himself and with a curt nod, turned his back to them as he swung around in his chair.

Thus dismissed, Aaron and Lauren stood up and left the office, not speaking until they reached the hallway.

"What was that all about, Aaron?" Lauren asked him in a low tone.

"I'm not sure, Lauren. I'm really not sure. He doesn't get involved as a rule, so I'm not sure what the hell is biting his ass this time. Where are you with the case?"

"Aaron, I don't have the time right now. We'll talk tonight at home. Monica called and something has her hysterical. I have a filing due in twenty minutes and I sure as hell didn't need Anderson's big nose in my business right now. See you tonight," she said in a dismissive tone, leaving him standing in the hall, perplexed.

She arrived at her office to see Justin smiling with reassurance. He had come through, just as she knew he would. She flew to her desk and quickly researched the remaining information and went into the system to find that Justin had already filled in his part. She clicked the button to file with less than a minute to spare, grabbed her purse and headed out the door.

"Betsy, I'm gone for the day," she said curtly and nodded at Justin as she left.

Lauren pulled into Monica's drive and noted that Nikki was already there, as promised. She found them in the living room. Monica was visibly shaking and Nikki had her arm over Monica's shoulders. She gave Lauren a roll of her eyes to indicate that she wasn't sure what was wrong and that it was bad.

Lauren threw down her bag and kicked off her shoes. "Okay, I'm here now; we're both here, Mon. What in hell has you so upset?"

Monica's voice was shuddering with breath between sobs. "Do you want some tea?" she asked in a hoarse voice.

"Fuck the tea," Nikki burst out. "Tell us what's going on."

"Okay, sit down and let me talk," Monica began, wiping her nose with a large piece of paper towel. The girls flopped down onto the sectional, preparing for the drama.

"Well, you know the room that's going to be a nursery?" Monica began. The others nodded, not wanting to interrupt because it always took Monica forever to tell her stories and she was not to be cheated of one moment of the self-pitying drama she loved so well.

"I've been asking Morgan to go get his boys checked," she started. "He won't do it. Just flat out refuses. You know I've been wantin' a baby so long and this just ain't happenin'," she continued, snuffing loudly, her crimson nails flashing in the balled up towel. "It just ain't been happenin'. My doc says there's no reason and it just takes time," she added.

"Mon, that's what I've been telling you all along," interjected Lauren despite Nikki's rolling eye warning not to interrupt.

"I know, I know, but the doc knows a little bit more about babies than you do, Lauren," Monica came back. Lauren flinched a little at this. The subject of having children was low on her priority list at the moment and she didn't need the reminder.

Monica kept talking, a fresh sob breaking out. "Well, I thought if I decorated the nursery, maybe it would sort of stimulate whatever needs stimulating in Morgan and me and maybe that's all it would take to get a baby cookin'," she explained. "So, I was in there this mornin', dragging boxes out of the closet to put in the attic." She burst out in a large, fresh sob and could hardly talk.

"Did you get hurt or something?" Lauren asked, perplexed.

"Jesus, Mon, spill it!" Nikki added.

Monica reached into the side of the sofa cushion where she was sitting and pulled out a sheet of white

165

paper. She held it out to Lauren, who, as the lawyer in the group, was given preference. Lauren took the paper and began to read it. "What is it?" demanded Nikki, bouncing over on the cushion to look over Lauren's shoulder.

Lauren's eyes grew as she read. "It appears to be a notification of filing for a paternity suit," she said and then dropped the paper into her lap. "It names Morgan as the alleged father," she concluded, looking at Nikki and then at Monica, who was crying inconsolably. "Mon? What's this all about?"

"You read it, didn't you?" Monica shrieked. "It means some bitch out there has been fuckin' my man and thinks he's the daddy of her bastard!"

The only sound for the next few minutes was Monica's wail. The other two sat there, trying to absorb what had been revealed and how this was going to impact Monica.

"Now, Mon, this is only a notice of filing. It's not a judge's decision." Lauren was trying to come up some sort of calming logic, but it wasn't easy. "Have you shown this to Morgan?" she asked hesitantly.

Monica shook her head. "He's not here. I don't know what to think or do," she cried.

Nikki stood up and went to stand next to Monica. "Well, it seems perfectly clear to me. When the bastard comes home, you ask him whose honeypot he's been dipping and why the fuck he hasn't told you about a baby! Don't give the bastard the benefit of the doubt, just accuse him right out! Don't give him time to think of some bullshit lie," she exploded in typical Nikki fashion.

Lauren wasn't in favor of such a confrontation, but considering what was going on in her own life, perhaps the direct approach would be better. "Mon, can you ask him tonight?" she asked tentatively.

Monica blew her nose. "You think I should?" she looked to Lauren for guidance.

Lauren felt a bit lost in this capacity. Monica was her best friend. She nodded at Monica, saying, "I agree with Nikki to a point. Ask him right out. You're not going to be able to hide this when he comes home, he'll see right through you. Just ask him in a calm, yes a calm voice," she added, looking pointedly at Nikki.

"Don't give him time to prepare a defense. Don't get nasty and don't scream. What's done is done. You just need the facts so you can decide calmly what you want to do about it."

Monica nodded, agreeing to the logic in Lauren's words. Lauren pulled out her phone and snapped a picture of the document. She would check it out when she got back into the office to see how the case ended up. She didn't let Monica see her doing this; it would have to be second in line to the Bartley case. What was done, was done.

Monica's eyes were on Lauren's face. "You are so lucky, Lauren. You and Aaron don't have these problems. You got a man you can depend on," she added.

Lauren just stared at Monica, unwilling to say a word. *If they only knew* she thought to herself. *If they only knew.*

CHAPTER TWENTY

Lauren left Monica's later that afternoon and headed out into the countryside to drive and think. Her life had become so confusing lately; she hadn't taken time to sort things out in her head, much less make the moves needed to resolve them.

Who was she to trust?

Her husband? She hardly recognized the man she had fallen in love with on that campus years before. He had withdrawn from her; that awful pacing throughout the night. The mysterious appearances in places he had no reason to be. She remembered that look on his face in Anderson's office; like a man who was about to drown. What was he hiding?

She loved her husband...still. Perhaps she loved the Aaron who had stood, strong and capable at the head of the lecture. Was it the man who had carried her over the threshold and made passionate love to her several times each night? He had been a stallion;

169

unquenchable and always ready. He'd brought her into the firm and she had felt immense pride and inflamed ambition at the possibilities of what they could accomplish together.

She knew Aaron still loved her; she could see it in his eyes. She knew he still desired her; she could see that in the outline of the pants, particularly when he wandered into her room to watch her dress or shower. Why didn't he simply grab her and throw her down upon the bed? Was it him... or was it her? Had she become unreachable, cold and distant to him? Was she shutting down her marriage intentionally, or out of an unwillingness to confront Aaron with her suspicions and resolve the matter? Was she willing to watch it simply drain away, like sand in an hourglass, until there was nothing left to salvage? The thought pained her. It would be a failure and that was something she would not entertain in her life. She was about success, accomplishment, and achievement of goals. Perhaps her marriage no longer was on that list?

She passed a tiny roadside park that overlooked the river and pulled in, getting out to sit on its bank. The current was strong from the recent storms and its turbulence drew her mentally into it. She could picture what it would feel like to be caught up in that rapid, churning water...unable to stay above the water and being hurled down against its bottom. That's what her life felt like right now.

Then there was Justin...sweet, romantic Justin. She had no idea what he was capable of, but from what she'd seen, it would be incredible. He had the looks, the brains, the money and the breeding to become anything he chose. Why had he chosen her? Was there a motive behind this? Could she trust him completely? What did he have to lose in being with her...or perhaps more to the point, what did he have to gain?

Anderson, well that one was easy to see. The obese pervert embodied everything that was abhorrent to her. She hated that part of herself that even wanted to work in his firm because with each win she accomplished, she made him a little richer and a little more cocky about what he had in his hen house of one.

How about the rest of the partners? They were mutants of Anderson, each a bit greedier than the last.

171

Her girls? They had their own lives and their own desires. They wouldn't betray her, but neither could they help her through this. A part of her understood Monica's desire to have children; it entered her mind from time to time as well, but then Aaron was not looking like father material at the moment. Lauren had to keep this uncertainty to herself; Monica's life was in an uproar and Lauren had to serve as her role model. Nikki, well Nikki was Nikki and while she took care of herself, Lauren didn't want her own personal trials to be a topic over tea and sandwiches.

She watched a flock of birds fly overhead and envied them. They flew in unison, always sure of where they were going and keeping the weak to the center where it could not be picked off by prey. Was she the weak one in the center, or was she at the rear...easily abandoned without a look back? The thought made her shudder and she thought about the Bartley case.

Bartley was as guilty as sin, but somehow she knew Anderson was setting him up for a fall. She could not let that happen. Was she smart enough to outwit a judge? Particularly one who had Anderson's

172

seal of approval? This was going to take everything she had in her bag of tricks. She hoped she could trust Justin; he was her ace in the hole.

CHAPTER TWENTY-ONE

Lauren drove home and found Aaron waiting for her in the living room. He was still dressed in his suit, reading the paper.

"Darling, I was hoping you'd be home soon," he greeted her with a kiss. "Touch up your hair, I'm taking you to dinner," he said cheerfully.

"Aaron, I don't know, it's been a long day…"

"Nonsense. We haven't been anywhere together in a very long time and that has to stop…now. After all, we're working on the case together and need to discuss details. Go on, get changed or whatever you're going to do and I'll wait right here for you. No arguments now."

Lauren sighed and nodded. They *did* need to go over the details of the case and it was much safer to do that without Justin sitting at the same table, so going to dinner would be a better idea. Secondly, she had to begin sorting out the mess she was in; she may as well begin at home.

Shortly thereafter they were speeding down the expressway in Aaron's silver Mercedes. Lauren had to admit that it felt good to be a wife for a change, to let down her guard and let Aaron be in control. Sometimes being so independent had it downsides.

Aaron took her to *L'Espalier*, the most expensive restaurant in town and well known for its French cuisine. He nodded to the headwaiter and they were promptly seated, ahead of those waiting with reservations. Lauren had to admit that being Aaron's wife had perks.

They were seated in a corner and this allowed them some privacy in discussion. Lauren was wearing a Liancarlo strapless black gown and looked stunning. Her hair was upswept and secured with a single diamond clasp. Her simplicity bespoke the elegance with which she presented herself—her signature style.

Aaron, looking strained, but cheerful, was overjoyed to have his wife to himself. He ordered champagne and requested the chef choose their meal personally. "How have you been, my darling?" he inquired as he poured the sparkling liquid into her flute.

"I'm well. Tired, but well, Aaron. How about you? You're not looking well and I'm concerned. Is something wrong?" she inquired with real empathy.

"Fine, fine," he said hurriedly and Lauren suspected he didn't want to dwell on the topic or else he might have to reveal details about who was keeping him up at night. She decided to let that topic lay and went on to another.

"Why did Anderson put you on the case?" she asked hoping to gain some insight into what was being planned behind her back.

"Came as a surprise to me, too, darling," he said, sipping. "As a matter of fact, I don't think he mentioned it to anyone before presenting it to you and I in his office. Much of what Mason does is done on whim, you know," he added.

Lauren nodded, still not satisfied. "But what does he think you bring to the table that I'm lacking?" she pressed.

"I suppose more experience. You are a bit young for the typical attorney assigned a case of this profile, you know." He looked at her across the candlelight to see her reaction.

Lauren sighed, "I suppose. I can't help but feel dirty when I leave his office. He has this way of making me feel like I'm a prostitute and he's my john," she observed. She looked at Aaron and saw his surprise. "I suppose that's hard for you to understand," she added.

"More like hard to stomach," he answered. "You are, after all, my wife. I don't want any man making you feel dirty. Has he ever made advances to you?" Aaron asked in a pinched voice.

"Anderson?" she scoffed. "Hell, no. He's gay, didn't you know? His wife was just a social convenience."

Aaron had the grace to look embarrassed. "Well, I won't say I've not heard that rumor from time to time, but nothing was ever confirmed."

"Women know these things, Aaron," she said, sipping her glass. "It's an instinct, don't you know?"

"Obviously not," he answered wryly. The waiter advanced with their first course and interrupted the conversation.

"You haven't answered my question, Aaron," Lauren reminded him.

"Oh? I thought I had. I really have no idea why, Lauren, but if I had to speculate I would say he's just a tad worried about your lack of experience. He knows you're sharp, has said as much, but Bartley is part of the ol' boys network and has to be protected," he observed.

Lauren thought about his and how it contrasted with Justin's opinion.

"So what is your strategy?" Aaron was asking.

Lauren considered how to answer and finally came out with the truth, at least most of it. "I get the idea that Bartley might not be as protected as you might think, Aaron. I think Anderson is setting me up for a fall. So, I'm looking for a loophole because I can't rely on the judge," she explained quickly, looking up at him to gauge his expression, which was curious.

"Why would he want Bartley to fall?" Aaron asked.

"You tell me," Lauren countered.

Aaron's brow was furrowed in deep thought. "Doesn't make sense," he said finally. "But I suppose not everything Mason does makes sense. I'm sure you know you're a possibility to replace him, Lauren," he went on.

"I doubt that," she answered. "I don't have enough, what did you call it, *experience*?"

"Don't be coy, Lauren. You know exactly how good you are and you're a beautiful, feisty woman who gets what she wants. That's powerful medicine in a courtroom and even more so over a panel of old fogies like myself who daydream of getting onto the golf course," he smiled.

"Old fogie? You? Aaron, come now. I'd say you're in your prime," she countered, surprised at herself for letting the conversation get to such a personal level.

179

"Nevertheless, your name has been whispered and perhaps Anderson isn't as keen on the idea as he should be. Maybe you represent a danger to him?" he suggested.

Lauren said nothing, thinking this over. It didn't sound like Aaron was holding anything back. If anything, he sounded more puzzled than she felt. Perhaps he wasn't behind all the tampering going on with the case. Perhaps he was truly on her side. But could she trust that?

They finished their dinner and before long, climbed back into Aaron's Mercedes and wheeled home. Once inside, Aaron turned and took Lauren into his arms. "Come to bed with me, darling," he begged, his eyes bright with desire.

She wanted to refuse; she had the crazy idea of telling him right then and there about Justin, but couldn't bring herself to do that. There were too many unanswered questions. So, she nodded.

Aaron loosed the zipper of her gown and it slid to the floor like a cascade of black stars. She was naked beneath and he drew in his breath at the sight of her standing here, just bare skin and spike heels. "You truly are magnificent, darling," he said, breathing hard.

Sliding off his jacket and slacks, he bent down on one knee and slid his hand up the inside of her thigh. His hand petted her there, one on each thigh, pushing them apart so his fingers could fondle her clit. Lauren's head rolled backward and she shut her eyes, but the picture she conjured was not of Aaron.

He lifted her and placed her on his bed, the satin quilted coverlet rippling the nerve endings on her sensitive flesh. He climbed over her, his mouth fastening down on her hardening nipples, his hands fondling her pussy with rhythmic circles that inflamed the tender flesh. He took her hands in his, then, and stretched them outward from her sides, as though she were on a cross. His lips began a trail of kisses from her fingertips, down to the soft flesh beneath her arms and then down her sides over her hip. Lauren's mind reeled with the pleasure of this subtlety.

Aaron was in full erection when he finally parted her legs completely, pulling her legs up to bend at the knee and sliding off the spiked heels. He entered her then and it was a thrust of defiance, almost as though it

181

would be his last. Lauren cried out at the sensual attack and she crossed her ankles behind his back, holding him inside as far as he reached. Her vagina pulsed around him, driving his pleasure beyond endurance.

"I love you, Lauren!" he cried out, pounding into her and holding her breasts in his hands. There were actually tears in the corners of his eyes and Lauren thought perhaps she was only seeing a reflection from the tiny nightlight across the room.

Aaron peaked just as Lauren climaxed and their combined juices flooded her, spilling out of her pussy and across the sheets. Spent, Aaron pulled out and fell, exhausted next to her. He seemed winded and was breathing heavily. Lauren wondered at this and it inspired the protectiveness in her to surface. She lifted his head and placed it against her breast, cuddling him to her as his breathing calmed. She smoothed his hair and kissed his forehead, whispering sounds of calming and comfort into his ear.

Aaron fell asleep like that, but Lauren lay awake for a very long time, wondering at what had just transpired. Amazingly, there she lay with her husband and yet she felt guilt toward Justin. She had told him that Aaron and she no longer slept together, and tonight had put an end to that. She wondered why Aaron seemed so fragile and needy; he had always been a man of primal strength.

Towards dawn Lauren maneuvered Aaron's head off her chest and onto a pillow. She slid away from him, gathered her gown and tiptoed out of his room into her own. She stood in the shower for a long time, letting the hot water cleanse her of guilt for sleeping with her own husband.

Exhausted, she then fell onto her own bed, dragging the sheet over herself and falling into a deep sleep.

It had begun.

CHAPTER TWENTY-TWO

Aaron was already gone when Lauren arose the next morning. His bed was neatly made, just like everything he did...neatly. She found a note on the kitchen counter next to the coffee pot; "Love You" it read. She couldn't help but smile, remembering the man she had fallen in love with. There was something different now, curiously fragile. It brought out the tender, protective side of her and for the time being, she decided to table any thinking resolutions with regard to Aaron. She felt instinctively that he needed her more than she needed him and while this puzzled her, she was content.

Checking her phone, she found messages from Nikki. Her voice sounded very, very drunk and there was a man laughing in the background, so Lauren ignored them. It would take the better part of a day for Nikki to sleep that one off.

She was more concerned that she hadn't heard anything further from Monica. *Damn that Morgan!*

She made a mental note to check into the papers she'd photographed with her phone. If she could find records on the cases, it might give Monica a little more light about what the hell was going on. In the meantime, Lauren drove past Monica's house on her way into the office. Everything looked normal and Lauren wasn't sure what she expected to see. She would call Monica after she'd done that research.

Lauren arrived in the office to find emptied desks and people standing in clusters, talking in low voices. Justin was not at his desk and even Betsy was nowhere to be found.

Lauren deposited her bag and briefcase in her office and set off to the partners' lounge to find out what was going on. She found Aaron there and gave him a brief, warm smile. Anderson was leaning in the corner; his corpulent body resting against the coffee bar and her smile to Aaron did not go unnoticed. He was smirking a bit and Lauren wondered what was behind that.

Walking to stand next to Aaron she asked him in an undertone, "What's going on?"

He shook his head slightly, indicating that he didn't want to discuss it at the moment. He turned and stood between Anderson and Lauren, keeping Anderson's gaze blocked. "I'll meet you in your office in thirty minutes," he said softly and then moved to stand and listen in on another group of others talking.

Lauren was completely baffled and after glancing at Anderson again, she left the room and returned to her office. She was torn between sitting to wait for Aaron and milling about among the other office employees to see what she could hear. However, as a partner, she should never let on that she wasn't in complete awareness and control of the situation and couldn't chance someone asking her a question she had no ability to answer. So, she waited.

Aaron appeared in her doorway about a half hour later and said, "Grab your coat, we're leaving," and Lauren nodded without argument and followed him.

They were soon in the Mercedes and it wasn't until they were out of the city that Aaron tapped the button to turn off the radio and said, "Shut down both our phones and bury them in the back seat under my coat." Lauren did as she was told but could feel a sense of alarm growing in the pit of her stomach. *Why all the mystery?*

As soon as she complied, Aaron left the expressway and headed down a country road, then another until he came to the river. He motioned to her to get out and they stood alongside the river's edge.

"Are you going to tell me what's going on?" she demanded. "Why all the cloak and dagger?"

"Lauren, I don't know who we can trust. Some heavy shit went down this morning before you got in. I can't get the full story but I do know it has to do with the Bartley case."

"The Bartley case? We haven't even gone to trial yet. What in the hell could be happening there?"

"You won the case," his words were brief and Aaron looked out over the river and compared the turbulence he was feeling with the rapid flowing current.

"Won the case? What in the hell are you talking about?" she demanded again.

"It's over!" he shouted. Aaron turned and looked at her full on, "It's over, do you understand? No more case, no more Bartley!" His face was flushed and yet pale at the same time. He staggered a bit and leaned against a tree for support.

Lauren shook her head, trying to process what she was seeing in his body language with the words he had just screamed at her. "Aaron..." she began.

"He's dead! Do you hear me? Bartley is dead! They found his body slumped over his desk last night. He blew his own head off, Lauren. He took a fucking gun and blew his goddamned head off!" Aaron shouted again. "God damnit!" he moaned, rubbing his hand along the side of his face.

Lauren's face was ashen and she sat down right where she'd stood, her expensive suit muddied and covered with leaves. "What are you talking about?" she pleaded in a whisper.

"Which part didn't you understand, my dear wife? Your client is dead. He killed himself. No client, no trial, no proof needed."

"But…" she started.

"But nothing, Lauren. But fucking nothing!" Aaron's voice was hoarse and he began coughing. Lauren barely heard him. All she could think of was the image of Bartley, his head exploded like a red pumpkin across his expensive desk. Her thoughts were spinning and then in one momentous second they cleared.

"Where is Justin?" she asked, her voice plaintive and suspiciously concerned.

"Who?" Aaron spat on the ground. "You mean the hunky paralegal you've been eyeballing for the last few weeks?"

Lauren's eyes opened wide. *What did he know or was he just guessing?* "He's the only other person who has been working on this case with me until you," she said calmly and rationally, using her best legal bypass the question technique.

"Don't pull that lawyer shit on me, Lauren. I *taught* you how to do that, don't forget. I know what I've seen and I'm not happy about it at all. As far as I know, you're still my wife and you'd better pray to God I don't get wind of something else because right now, I'm the most powerful friend you've got, my dear!" With that, Aaron turned and strode back toward the car.

Lauren stood then and faced the river for several minutes, her heart hammering. *Where is Justin? Why isn't he in the office this morning? Is he all right? Or could he even be involved in some way?* She knew Justin was too smart to get involved in setting up Bartley and then not showing up for work...too obvious. That left the first alternative and the mere thought of it scared her to death. Her knees began to shake and she was chilled. She recognized she was in trouble, especially after not having anything to eat this morning, so she turned and climbed back into the Mercedes with Aaron.

There was a long silence between them. Aaron finally broke it. "I don't want to know what has been going on, if anything," he began. "But it stops now, Lauren. It stops now." He turned and looked at her. "Look at me!" he barked.

Lauren turned and stared at his flushed face. Her knees continue to quiver. "I need food," she said. "I haven't eaten...the upset...I feel like I'm going to pass out," she whimpered and then lay her head back against the headrest and closed her eyes.

Aaron could see she was in trouble and without another word, he flipped the ignition and steered the Mercedes back onto the road with a squeal of the tires. They came to a min-mart and he pulled in and disappeared inside. Shortly thereafter he was back in the car and handed her a bottle of orange juice. "Drink this," he ordered and uncapped it for her.

Lauren took the bottle and slowly began to sip it. It felt thick in her throat and burned, but she needed the sugar. Her knees continued to shake.

"Eat this," Aaron commanded and handed her some turkey luncheon meat he pulled out of a vacuum-sealed bag. "You need protein."

Lauren nodded and accepted the meat. Aaron handed her some paper napkins and then turned on the car and flipped on the heat. He sat while she ate, his fingers tapping the top of the steering wheel. He was deep in thought and left her alone for the moment so she could recover.

Lauren began to feel a bit warmer and her knees stopped shaking. With every breath she could feel the fog in her brain clearing and as it did, the alarm she felt about Justin's whereabouts increased. She couldn't vocalize this, however. Aaron was in no mood to sympathize. Perhaps it would be safer to not mention Justin for now...there was nothing she could do one way or another but pray for his safety.

She realized Aaron was speaking.

"You have gotten involved in something without knowing it," he began, and she knew he was not referring to Justin. "You're in deep shit, Lauren, and they were about to send me to the bottom with you. They must have run out of time."

Lauren thought about this and she finally spoke up. "Are you saying the partners had something to do with this?"

"I'm not saying anything, Lauren," he snapped in a harsh tone. "But I'm nobody's fool, no matter what they may think," he said and turned to look at her directly in a double entendre.

Lauren bit back the words and the worry. Aaron snapped on the ignition and guided the Mercedes back onto the road. Soon they were back on the expressway and Aaron pulled into the parking garage behind Lauren's car. "Go home for the rest of the day, Lauren," he said in a quiet voice. "Lock the doors and don't open it to anyone. I'll go back up and see what I can find out." His voice was solemn and did not invite any argument.

Lauren offered none, but opened her door and climbed out. Aaron rolled down the power window. "Lauren..." he said. She turned and leaned in the window. "Don't worry, darling. I love you and we'll get through this. There are more important things and this will pass. Just be alert and don't trust *anyone*," he said, emphasizing the "anyone."

Lauren smiled somewhat and nodded, then turned and got into her car. Aaron pulled into a parking place and she watched as he headed to the elevator.

She checked her phone...nothing from Justin. She said a prayer and started the engine, heading home.

CHAPTER TWENTY-THREE

Lauren was napping fitfully when Aaron came home that night. It was late, very late, and she didn't want to retire until she'd talked to him. She tried not to assume he'd been out with another woman, but it was hard to rule that out entirely. After all, he had suggested that she and Justin had something more between them than a professional relationship and yet hadn't seemed to get too irate at the idea. Why was that?

She heard the door open downstairs and came down the staircase, her hair loose and tousled. Aaron looked up at her and his heart swelled with love for the woman he saw. *She doesn't deserve this* he thought to himself.

"Hi," he called to her. She smiled and came down, pulling her robe tightly around herself. "C'mon in the living room, let's talk," he said. Lauren nodded and followed him in to take a seat on the sofa, sitting sideways and pulling her legs beneath herself. He smiled and thought how she always looked like a child when she did that. It was endearing.

"So, what did you find out?" she asked, her eyelids puffy from sleeping.

"Not much," he answered, sitting down in the wingback and lighting his pipe. She waited while he tamped it, taking some deep breaths and then releasing the smoke into the air above him. Lauren hated his pipe smoking, but tolerated it because it wasn't worth the argument.

"Tell me everything," she prompted.

"Well," he took another deep breath, "we were notified by court order to freeze all proceedings having to do with his case. The records are to be sealed and no one may have access to them until a judge has seen them." Aaron shifted his legs as though still uncomfortable in the chair. "Pretty much what I expected."

"But the partners, Anderson...what are they saying?"

"Well, darling, that's the part you're not going to be very fond of," he said softly. Lauren sat up, waiting for whatever bomb was about to fall.

"What is it?" she asked wryly.

"I may as well tell you straight out. Anderson has planted a seed among the partners to suggest that Bartley may have felt, well, "under-represented" and that could have contributed to his depression and consequent suicide." Aaron waited for the explosion.

"What? Are you fucking kidding me?" came the explosion. "What does he mean 'under-represented'? Who the fuck does he think he has on the case? Justin, you and me for Christsakes!" Lauren was so incensed that she neglected to note that she mentioned a paralegal before two experienced attorneys. Aaron did notice.

"Well, of course, darling Lauren. How could Bartley imagine that when he had *Justin* on his side?" he mocked her wryly. He put his pipe into the ashtray, stood and flipped off the lamp on the table. "Goodnight, Lauren," he said softly and slowly went up the stairs to his bedroom. Lauren heard his door shut with a slightly louder than normal *click*.

Wonderful! she thought.

Monica wasn't one to sit back and let life take her over; she took over life. She didn't know why Lauren hadn't gotten back to her on the papers she'd found, but she suspected something out of the ordinary was going on in Lauren's life right now. She thought she'd give Lauren a call later although she doubted there was anything she could do. Lauren, like her, was an independent woman and perfectly capable of taking care of herself.

Monica had hired an attorney. Jorgensen was his name and he came with a high price tag but Morgan would be paying for it, so Monica didn't care. Jorgensen was looking into things and in the meantime, Monica began looking for a place to hide money. She withdrew up to her limit without triggering an IRS form each day and put it in a rented storage locker. She didn't care how safe it was; anywhere was safer than in an account with Morgan's name on it.

She went by the Goodwill and bought armloads of the newest looking clothes she could find. These were strewn across her bed, making it look like she'd been out shopping. Morgan saw these and made comments that she was going to break the bank. She simply laughed and said she was depressed because she wasn't getting pregnant and she may as well make herself beautiful for him in the meantime.

Monica rented a post office box and had all her mail forwarded there. She applied for every credit card Morgan's credit would allow and had the statements sent to the PO Box. Then she borrowed cash on each card to its limit and this, too, went into that blue shoebox in the golf bag of the storage locker.

She went into Morgan's email accounts and set them all up to copy automatically to her, incoming and outgoing. This way she could track everyone he wrote with. She called the cell phone company and ordered a new phone with account for herself and added a special service to Morgan's account that let her track every telephone call and text he took part in.

She got the documents she'd found in the would-be nursery and put them in the golf bag with the money. If Jorgensen came back with what she expected, she would be ready.

CHAPTER TWENTY-FOUR

Lauren barely slept that night. She had nightmares of making love with a man who possessed Justin's body and Aaron's face. The man was gentle and loving one moment and ardently powerful the next. There were no exact parallels; neither creature was true in character.

She sat up finally about four in the morning, flipped on her nightstand light and went into the bathroom to splash cold water on her face and hopefully rid herself of the garbled dreams. She hated nights like these; especially when sleeping alone. She longed to climb under the covers with Aaron and simply be held and comforted. But Aaron's sudden coldness when they had talked probably lay behind the nightmare and she doubted whether he was in a comforting mood.

She gave up as the sun rose and drowned her misery in a hot bath before dressing to go to the office.

She wanted a first-hand grasp of what was going down; otherwise it felt too much like being a victim.

She wore her double-breasted navy blue suit with a crisp, white blouse and diamond stud earrings. This was a day for dressing with authority. When she arrived, Betsy looked up with that doe-in-the-headlights expression and instantly Lauren's radar popped up. Justin's desk was empty and Lauren motioned toward it with a questioning look on her face. Betsy shrugged and quickly looked down at whatever she was reading.

Lauren went in to her desk and saw the reason. There was an envelope of crisp stationery lying there. Her name was typed on its face, but it was otherwise unidentifiable. She looked out at Betsy who was very purposefully trying to avoid her.

Lauren picked up the envelope and turned it around between her fingers a few times, considering who it might be from and what it held. As an attorney she was tempted to not even open it as that constituted receipt and acknowledgement. Sometimes things were better left unacknowledged.

She strolled out toward Betsy's desk and said, "Judging by how hard you're trying not to catch my eye, I'm guessing you know who this is from and don't want to say?"

Betsy looked up and shook her head. "It was there when I came in, Lauren. I've never seen anything similar so I have no idea who it's from, I'm sorry." She saw the confusion on Lauren's face and added, "Perhaps it's not my place to say, but I'm guessing whomever is behind it doesn't mean you any harm. Those people wouldn't have written a note; they would have just ordered you into their office," she offered, looking down the hall in the direction of Anderson's door.

Lauren nodded and went back to her chair, guessing that Betsy was probably right. Hoping it was somehow from Justin, she slipped the envelope into her purse, to be read later when she had more privacy.

She brought up the computer then and chanced looking for anything she could find on the Bartley case. The records were there but were password-protected and she couldn't access them. She buzzed Betsey and was told no one in the firm could get to them except with a court order. Lauren nodded and felt a little desperate. It was like being hunted but not seeing who was after you.

Betsy buzzed her then and announced that a partners' meeting had been called in the conference room immediately. Lauren said, "Be sure Aaron is notified," hoping her only ally was in by now and ready to stand behind her.

Lauren's palms were perspiring so she grabbed her laptop even though there was nothing there to work on now that the Bartley case was in limbo. At least it would give her something to occupy her time and have an excuse to avoid Anderson's fire-eyed stare. When she entered the conference room, Aaron was nowhere to be seen so she poured a cup of coffee and took a place at the far end of the table from Anderson. To her immense relief, just as Anderson walked in, so did Aaron, and he sat down beside her. There was a palpable tension in the room as the partners had already begun to choose sides.

Anderson cleared his throat and began with some perfunctory comments about attendance in the office and needing to stir up new business now that one major client was no longer in the system.

Lauren knew the comments were directed at her but she pretended to be completely casual, even nodding in agreement. Then Anderson shot the cannon ball over her bow.

"As most of you know, the late Mr. Bartley, God rest his soul, is no longer with us as a result of his own hand. It has been suggested among his peers that perhaps our firm was in some way responsible." He paused to clear his throat and around the table, the men were giving Lauren sidelong glances surreptitiously.

Lauren knew the time had come to marshal her forces or lie dead in the water. "Mr. Anderson, I'm sure you realize what a ridiculous rumor that is and that the full weight of each of the partners will be applied to put an end to it immediately."

"Is it?" Anderson shot the next cannon ball. "How would you explain his lack of confidence in our firm then, Mrs. Reynolds?"

"Perhaps that is a question better posed to you directly, Mr. Anderson," she countered. "After all, you seemed to be a trusted friend and advisor and it was with your support that Aaron, Justin and I were assigned to his case. Surely you understood your full intentions for doing that?" Lauren dared.

Anderson's face turned an even deeper shade of mottled burgundy. "It seems my confidence was misplaced," he shot back.

Lauren stared at him and was reminded of a misshapen beet, recently pulled from the muddy ground. His face was hideous in anger. "Perhaps it was the client's confidence that was misplaced," she uttered and looked him straight in the eyes.

There was a subtle noise in the room as the partners shifted uneasily in their chairs and she felt Aaron kick her beneath the conference table.

Lauren's resolve was not shaken, however. She knew Anderson would take no prisoners and if she was going to go down in flames, she would not do it silently.

206

"And just where is the good Mr. Wilder this morning, Mrs. Reynolds? Has he gotten off his leash?" Anderson snarled.

Lauren could feel her face burn and Aaron's eyes on her as well. "Mr. Wilder has not contacted the office with his whereabouts, Mr. Anderson. I had rather hoped you might be able to shed some light on the matter?" Lauren felt ruthless and defiant. She was running on pure adrenalin and knew at some point Anderson's mighty paw would reach out and smash her flat...but she did not back down.

"Is that so?" Anderson countered. "Well, I was misinformed then because I understood that Mr. Wilder left you some written communication just this morning." He smiled oh so slightly as he played his hidden ace.

Lauren blanched, realizing then that Anderson was behind the note and had just given himself away. "There was indeed an envelope on my desk this morning, Mr. Anderson, but I never opened it so I have no idea who it was from. You, on the other hand, seem to not only know its author, but possibly its contents?"

It was Anderson's turn to pale now as he realized he had just stepped into his own bear trap. The partners shifted in their chairs again, like tiny soldiers leaning toward Lauren subconsciously in a sign that she had won. Lauren rejoiced inside and she felt Aaron's tension at her side. Anderson, however, was not yet done.

"I will not have such impertinence in these offices!" he shouted.

"Neither will I, Mr. Anderson," Lauren said quietly but everyone heard her. "Neither will I."

CHAPTER TWENTY-FIVE

Monica watched from her bedroom window as Morgan's car pulled into the drive. There was a message from Jorgensen on her cell, but she hadn't had the courage to listen to it yet.

There were warring emotions she was feeling; on one hand she felt betrayed and angry, wanting to confront Morgan and to let the bodies fall where they may. The other part of her wanted to forget she'd found those papers and to simply go back to their lives, untouched by the past.

There was one huge question that hung over them, however...was whatever happened truly in the past?

Monica wanted a baby with Morgan. She loved him and he was everything she desired in the father of her child. What about that other child, though?

She heard the door open downstairs and Morgan's voice called out, "Babe, I'm home!" Monica started down the stairs to see him. She had been rehearsing this scene for a very long time and her knees felt weak from the anticipation of what was about to come. Morgan was her entire life. Was life, as she knew it, about to end?

Morgan was standing in the foyer, all 6 feet 4 inches of him. Monica's heart fluttered yet again. His eyes were bright with desire to see her and his smile flashed as he held out his arms. "C'mere baby," he leaned forward to scoop her up and took her into the living room.

Morgan laid her on the sofa and knelt on the floor next to it. "What have you been doin' all day, baby?" he asked, his hands sliding up the length of her legs.

Monica squirmed and the heat rushed into her belly. "I missed you," she said honestly, although perhaps not quite as he believed she meant it.

He was encouraged, though, and began to slide down the jeggings she wore, his fingers hooking into her panties at the same time. Soon he had her naked from the waist down but before he would allow himself to touch her, he lifted her enough to unfasten her bra and slid it out from beneath her shirt. She felt almost more than totally exposed and it felt delicious!

Morgan used one hand to separate her legs, bending one at the knee and pushing it back into the sofa cushions. The other knee he pulled toward himself; the effect was that Monica was splayed openly and her nipples pushed against the fabric of her blouse in the most beckoning manner. Morgan slid one hand up her leg and into her moist clit, massaging it lightly with his index finger. She moaned, her head rolled backward and he took advantage of this to push her shirt up just enough to expose one ruby red nipple. His mouth came down upon it, suckling gently while he continued to roll and fondle her swelling clit. Monica attempted to roll away from him, the pleasure too overwhelming, but he held her in place with firm, sensual insistence. "Just feel it, baby," he whispered and this made her even more turned on.

He came down upon her with his mouth then; feeding upon her as if starving for her juices. She cried out at the delicious sensation of his attack and arched her pelvis to push herself further into his mouth. Her hand fumbled at his belt and zipper and soon, he, too, was naked from the waist down.

Morgan reached beneath her bottom and lifted her high into the air and then kicked cushions down onto the carpet where he deposited her. He pushed her knees wide and took her with a powerful, deep thrust.

"Sweet Jesus!" she cried out, her eyes rolling upward behind her eyelids. Morgan drove into her, over and over, each time more possessive than the last. Monica could feel herself reaching that trigger where the world becomes stars and she dug her nails into Morgan's back.

Morgan's voice penetrated her sensual fog as he came into her, hot and flooding. It was a sound of triumph, of possession; the sort men make when they've conquered a foe.

They lay that way a long time, layered and sweating upon the carpet and cushions. Monica's body was quivering with the exhaustion and release of what had just happened. She also had tears welling into her beautiful eyes. They spilled onto her cheeks and her shoulders lightly shivered with the emotion she was feeling.

"Mon, what it is, darling?" Morgan pushed up and looked down at her. "Why are you crying?"

Monica looked at him, her lips quivering and her face ravished with pain. "I know..." she whispered finally.

Morgan stiffened and then caught himself with a practiced posture. "Know what?" he asked, his voice no longer tender, but guarded.

Monica said nothing, but lay there with her pain pouring from her eyes and her heart. She felt supremely naked; not only in reality, but in the way Morgan could read her mind. He knew what she was talking about.

His face closed and he rose to sit, holding his head in his hands and turning away from her. It was all she needed to know. She didn't need a message from the detective; she didn't need an opinion from Lauren...she needed only to look at Morgan's bent back to know everything she suspected was true.

213

"It didn't mean anything," he said in a low voice.

Monica stood then, naked and vulnerable, but her chin lifted. "That's exactly what I was afraid you would say," she whispered. "Because if she meant nothing to you, and you still had a baby with her, but you won't with me…what does that make me?"

Morgan looked up at her, his semen still dripping down the inside of her thigh, and knew in that moment there was no way back. There was nothing he could say, nothing he could undo. The judge, the jury and his punishment stood before him, prideful and devastated. He would never, in his entire life, forget the picture of Monica as she hesitated in pose that one last moment…and then silently walked past him, up the stairs, and out of his life.

CHAPTER TWENTY-SIX

Lauren was already home when Aaron came in. He had a passive look on his face but she knew him well enough to recognize that didn't necessarily mean he was in a good mood.

He waited until they were seated at dinner. Lauren had prepared grilled salmon steaks with asparagus and a tossed salad. She'd set the table with wine goblets, hoping to make a rather festive occasion out of the day. Aaron was not impressed.

His voice was quiet, chastising. "What did you think you were doing with that little performance you staged?" he began. "Don't you realize who Anderson is? Don't you know you, hell even I, could disappear tomorrow and no one would ask any questions?"

"Don't lecture me, Aaron. I'm not one of your students any more," she added with an acidic tone.

"No, you've gone quite beyond that, my dear. In fact, you've gone quite mad. You may very well have demolished your career with that little episode," he finished as he stabbed the salmon with considerably more force than was necessary.

Lauren was thoughtful. She was wearing a paisley caftan with gold sandals and looked quite lovely there in her concentration. Aaron's heart melted; he did love her so, but she made it so damned hard to protect her!

"I can't let Anderson make me his lap dog, Aaron, I just can't," she murmured.

Aaron slammed down his fork. "Damnit, Lauren! You can and you *will* do whatever it takes to keep your career. You're no stranger to defending the guilty; it's part of the job, and you know it. Anderson is just like a guilty client. He pays your salary and holds the strings. One word from him and you'll be disbarred for some phony reason, if not sent to prison." Aaron was very angry and it was motivated by his desire to keep her safe. "Look," he went on a bit more calmly. "There is the law and there is Anderson and don't think the two are on the same side. Do you know what I'm saying, Lauren?"

"Yes, yes, of course I do! That's why I won't bow down! Can't you see that? Can't you see that there's more than my reputation at stake here?"

"Yes, Lauren, I can. You're right. There is more than your reputation at stake...there is your very life, if not mine. We've come too far, worked too hard to throw it all away now on some hissy fit," he added.

"Hissy fit?" her eyes flamed. "Is that what you think this is? Some feminist stand?" Lauren unfairly turned her frustration on Aaron, but he had stuck the bear with a stick. "Aaron, if I don't stand my ground, Anderson will own me. I will be a piece in his chess game and my life will not be my own! All the work I've put in, all the education, all of it; will belong to him, not me. I want my own life, Aaron. I'm not going to sit in his lap and lick his limp dick when he orders it. I won't do it, Aaron, and you can't ask me to." Lauren stood and picked up her dishes, scraping most of her dinner into the garbage. Her shoulders were shaking and Aaron recognized she was crying. He felt badly; he should have supported her. It meant everything to her.

Aaron stood and went up to Lauren as she stood at the sink, her frail shoulders shaking. He leaned forward and wrapped his arms around her, kissing the back of her neck. "There, there, darling, I was too rough on you, I know that now. I'm sorry. I just don't want you harmed and you are your own greatest enemy. You know I stand behind you and will protect you with my dying breath," he whispered into her hair. Lauren shuddered a bit as women who have been crying hard can do. Aaron's hands crossed and gradually slid into the folds of her caftan, cupping the bare breasts inside.

Lauren's knees gave way then and she turned to face him, her eyes huge and magnified with the tears. Aaron thought in that moment he had never seen her look more fragile, more vulnerable and he couldn't help himself. His hands tore open the caftan and slid it off her slim shoulders. She was naked beneath, as he knew she would be.

Aaron put his hands on her waist and lifted her up to sit on the cooking island. He took her chin in his hands and kissed her deeply, probing the inside of her mouth with his tongue. Her tongue answered and effect made him harder than he could remember being in years. He bent low and gently pulled her legs apart, then pulled her toward his waiting mouth. "Don't move," he whispered, his eyes focused on her beautiful clit. "This is mine and it won't sit on anyone lap, but mine," he declared, his mouth going down on her.

Aaron's fingers opened her wide to his view and his tongue began flicking the tender skin he had exposed. Lauren uttered an animal sound and lifted her legs until they were almost vertical over her head. She gave him full entry into her very core and he wasted no time.

Aaron ripped the buttons off his shirt as he frantically pulled it over his head. His belt and pants were gone moments later and he pulled Lauren's pulsing womanhood toward himself, thrusting in and against her bottom with such a force that she now sat her weight entirely upon him. He filled her with himself and would not let her go. It was an act of desperation, of need, of dominance.

He lifted her from the counter and laid her upon the kitchen floor, cradling her head gently as she landed. With a ferocity that was almost animal, he pounded into her, over and over as Lauren arched upward to meet him. Just before he was about to spill his seed, Lauren pushed him off and rolled to climb atop him. Her mouth came down on him, sucking the throbbing rod that threatened to burst. "Give it all to me, Aaron. I want it!" she cried and he exploded into her mouth, a wild cry of triumph ripping from his throat. Before he was totally spent, Lauren flew to seat herself upon his hardness; that his sperm could fill her deep and hot. "Now, Aaron, give it to me now!" she screamed, no longer content to be dominated. All the anger, all the frustration, all the need had culminated in this challenge of sexual battle. She felt Aaron's orgasm and matched him; the rhythm of time immemorial.

When the spasms subsided, Lauren rolled to Aaron's side and lay there on the cold kitchen floor, nestled into his arm, and cried.

The cell was vibrating on Lauren's nightstand and she fumbled for it in her exhausted sleep. Nikki's face identified the caller and Lauren tapped the phone's face.

"Hello?" she answered in a sleep-dulled voice.

"Lauren?" Nikki's voice was high-pitched and frightened. "Lauren, help me!"

Lauren sat up now and tapped the phone's speaker so Aaron, who was lying next to her, could hear. "Nikki? Nikki? What's wrong? Where are you?"

"Lauren, please help me, I need you," Nikki's voice was strange and almost singsong. "The Hilton, Lauren. Ask for David Smith and come straight up. I don't know what room I'm in. Please hurry, Lauren, please hurry."

"Nikki, are you all right?" Lauren pleaded, but the phone had gone silent. She looked at Aaron who was already throwing back the blankets and headed to his closet.

"Get dressed," he ordered and Lauren wasted no time in complying.

Five minutes later they were speeding down the residential streets, headed for the expressway and downtown. Lauren had a cold feeling of dread and considered calling Monica but knew if anyone could help Nikki, it would be most likely she, Lauren, who would be best positioned.

She only hoped they wouldn't be too late.

CHAPTER TWENTY-SEVEN

Aaron and Lauren entered the Hilton through the brass revolving doors and Lauren pushed the elevator button while Aaron secured a room number from the front desk. They found the room easily and Aaron knocked while Lauren called out, "Nikki, it's Lauren and Aaron, open up!"

There was a noise from within, a sort of whimper, and full minutes passed before the door clicked open. Lauren pushed in and was heartbroken by what she saw.

The room was in shambles, lamps overturned, television ripped from the wall and even bath towels were torn in half and soaking up urine in the bathroom doorway. The odor was repulsive, but not nearly as horrifying as the vision of Nikki.

She sat naked on the corner of the bed, its mattress stained with fresh blood amidst huge chunks of the batting shredded as if with a knife.

"My God, Nikki!!! Are you okay? Who did this? Aaron, call an ambulance!"

Aaron turned out of respect for Nikki's appearance and pulled out his phone.

"Put it away, Aaron, please," Nikki pleaded. "It's not what it looks like."

"What do you mean?" Lauren shrieked. "How could it not be?"

"Aaron, I love you for coming, but would you mind waiting downstairs in the bar or something? I need to talk to Lauren alone." Nikki's voice was stronger and she wasn't asking.

Aaron looked doubtful; his phone still in his hand, but Lauren took one look at the expression on Nikki's face and then turned to Aaron, "Go ahead. Go to the desk and find us an empty room on this floor, please?"

Aaron hesitated a moment more, nodded and after sticking his head into the horrific bathroom to look for the culprit, he left and quietly shut the door behind himself.

"Where are your clothes, Nikki?" Lauren asked, looking around. The most immediate need she felt was to get out of the piss and destruction in this room. There was plenty of time to talk after they were comfortable.

Nikki pointed to a pile on the floor beneath the desk chair. "What's left of them is over there."

Lauren kicked aside the chair and picked up pieces of clothing that were stained and torn. There was a coat at the bottom of the pile that seemed to be intact so she held it toward Nikki and ordered, "Put this on, darling."

Lauren's phone buzzed; it was a text from Aaron. "Room 651. Will meet you at the door."

"C'mon Nikki," Lauren cooed, "Aaron has a room that's all nice and clean down the hall for us. Let's go get cleaned up and figure out what this is all about."

Nikki nodded and got to her wobbly feet, taking the arm Lauren offered. They followed the room numbers until they came to 651, just as Aaron hurried up behind them. He slid in the key card and opened the door, standing back for them to enter.

Aaron had secured a suite for them; two very large bedrooms with on suites and a sitting room that tied these together. Lauren directed Nikki to one of the baths and turned on the water for a hot shower. "Can you manage to shower on your own, darling?" Nikki nodded. "Then take your time. I'll be waiting outside." With that, she left Nikki and met Aaron in the sitting room.

"What the hell happened?" was his outburst as she entered.

Lauren held up a finger to delay him as she tapped her cell. "Hello? Yes, this is Lauren Reynolds in 651. I'd like an assortment of ladies clothing, size 6, to be delivered to my room immediately. Lingerie... something soft and comforting for an outing and a coat. Oh, and add some sunglasses. Yes, that's right. No, I don't care about style, just aim for comfort. Now, please, thank you." She tapped the phone off and threw herself into a side chair. "Is there something to drink in that bar?"

Aaron nodded, "I agree," he said and went to fetch them something. He found orange juice and split a tiny bottle of vodka between the glasses. He held out one to Lauren and took a chair himself. "What's going on? Did she tell you anything?"

Lauren shook her head and took a deep sip of the drink. The sugar and the alcohol were needed to ward off the shaking of her knees and the unsettled stomach from the disgusting mess in the other room. "I have no idea. Let's just get her cleaned up and dressed; then we'll find out."

Aaron nodded and flipped on a music channel from the television. They both leaned back and relaxed.

Nikki finally emerged, her hair wrapped in a towel, wearing the coat over her nakedness. At the same moment, there was a knock on the door and Aaron answered it to find a porter standing there with a rack of clothing. "The manager directed me to bring these up and let the lady choose," he said curtly. Aaron tipped him, nodded and slid the rack inside the door.

"Nikki? These are for you, honey," he said in a gentle voice.

"You guys are being entirely too good to me," Nikki said, crossing to the rack and rifling through the selections.

"Nonsense," said Lauren. "Get dressed, darling, and we'll sort this all out.

Nikki made her selections and disappeared into the bedroom for a few minutes, emerging with damp, finger-combed hair and a scrubbed look on her face. Lauren handed her a comb and waited. Aaron sprang up to make Nikki a drink as well and eventually Nikki was situated in her own club chair.

"Are you hurt anywhere?" Lauren began.

Nikki shook her head. "No…. the blood you saw was from my period. Sorry, Aaron, but no good way to put it." Aaron nodded, a bit flushed and even more puzzled.

"Who was he?" Lauren asked the obvious.

Nikki emptied her drink and held out the glass for another. Aaron obliged and she up-ended that one as well.

"Enough for now, Nikki," Lauren said quietly. I want you sober for this."

"I don't know who he was, Lauren, but he seemed to know you," she said, looking Lauren directly in the eye.

Lauren's eyes grew large, "Me? What are you talking about?" She heard Aaron's muttered curse behind her but ignored him for the moment.

"He told me to ask you to come and get me." The statement was flat and without humor. Nikki wasn't kidding.

"Nikki, tell me what the fuck is going on here. I'm not going to drag it out of you in delicate little bits. There's a clock ticking, a room destroyed and a woman in front of me who has clearly had better nights. Tell me!" Lauren ordered, out of patience with Nikki's normal dramatics.

"Okay, Lauren, I *will* tell you, but sit there and shut up."

Lauren's body slumped back into her chair in disgusted defeat. She motioned with her hand to indicate that Nikki had the stage.

Nikki closed her eyes and began speaking. She was not afraid of who she was and seldom explained her behavior. "I came in here last night, was...well, let's say I'm still trying to find myself. I sat at the bar and about an hour later as I was talking to this really nice guy, David, who came in and took the next seat... anyway, this big guy, old fart, comes in and walks up to us. He didn't even look at David; David just tipped up the rest of his drink, swung around and left. I thought that was kind of weird, but figured maybe the big guy was someone David didn't want to piss off." Nikki was not known for short sentences or getting to the point any time soon. Lauren knew this and also knew it was futile to rush her; she would tell in her own time. "So," Nikki went on, "This old fart sits in David's chair but doesn't order a drink. He pulls out this pipe and fiddles with it a while and then lights it. So, I say, 'No smoking in here, pal' and he just chuckles and continues to puff."

Lauren felt a cold rush of blood and heard Aaron curse again behind her. She nodded to Nikki to go on.

"So this asshole old fart sits there puffing for a while and when I turned to leave, he grabbed my arm under the bar and his fingers dug into my skin. Then he reaches into his pocket and slides a packet and a key card into my hand. I said, 'What's that?' and he says, 'David is waiting for you, room 602.' So, I'm like, *cool!* I get a little powder and I don't have to sleep with the old fart to party." Nikki paused for breath and ignored Lauren's rolling eyes.

Aaron was growling under his breath in frustration and he got up to make himself another drink. Lauren barked, "Aaron, don't. You know where this is going and you need to stay sober." Aaron stopped in his tracks and he agreed by sitting back down. His expression had lost compassion for Nikki, though.

"Then what happened?" Lauren asked quietly, dreading what she knew was coming.

"So, I take the key card and the packet and head up here. I opened the door and there was David, sitting on the bed, so I went in. But then there's another guy sitting in a chair in the shadows and I think, "Oh, great, a pair of screws." Nikki laughed now as she remembered the excitement that had tingled in her at the thought. "But the other guy didn't look horny; he looked tough, you know? David smiled and held out his hand to me, so I went over and when he reaches out, he starts to tear off my clothes. So, I think, 'Cool!' he's the caveman type. I tell him, 'Hey buddy, I'm on the rag, you know?' He didn't seem to care and kept taking off my clothes. The guy in the corner gets out his phone and starts taking pictures of me. David holds out a glass with a blade and motions for me to put the powder on it. The guy keeps snappin' those damned pictures. This starts to feel bad, so I stop and start pickin' up my clothes. The guy in the corner snaps open a switchblade and I'm like, 'Holy shit, this is screwed up.' I hollered at the guy in the corner to stay out of my way and he gets all pissy and in my face, holding the blade up to my tits. Now, Lauren, you know I'm not goin' take that shit, so I used one of the moves Stanley...did I ever tell you about the martial arts guy, Stanley?"

Lauren said, "Get on with the story!"

232

"Shit! Girl! Okay, okay... So I used a move Stanley taught me and snapped this guy's wrist so he dropped the knife and I picked it up. He backed up and was really pissed...I think I mighta broke his wrist...but he starts toward the door and I turn and David is sitting there, about ready to shit. So, I climb on to the bed and start carving up the covers and the mattress...letting him know I mean business. Then I started throwing things, like the lamps and I even pissed on the bathroom floor. It's like I completely went Ninja, you know? David gets this 'oh shit' look and jumps around me to the door. They open it and there's the fat asshole standing there. The guy in the corner hands him the phone and takes off somewhere. The fat asshole sticks his head in and says real hoarse-like, "Tell Lauren to come and rescue you now.' Who the hell was he, Lauren?"

Lauren's eyes were closed and Aaron was already on his feet. "We're leaving, now!" Aaron ordered and then forced Lauren to stand. "Nikki, we'll drop you at home, but you pretty much just fucked up Lauren's entire life. You didn't know what the fuck you were playing with, but I can assure you, you'd better clean

233

up your act because your ass is hanging out right about now."

Lauren's face was pale and her knees wobbly. "Aaron?" she managed and then slid to the floor in a faint. Aaron scooped her up and took her into the other bedroom, ordering Nikki to get some cool cloths. He sat next to Lauren's side on the bed until she revived. He handed her a glass with bourbon he'd found in the bar.

"Drink this," he ordered and there was no argument. When her face seemed more normal, Aaron took her by the hand and headed out the door, Nikki left standing behind, her mouth gaping. Aaron stopped, whipped a hundred dollar bill out of his wallet and tossed it in Nikki's direction. "Find a way home," he barked and they left.

Downstairs they climbed into his car and Aaron roared off to the expressway. "Don't say a word," he ordered. "The game has just jumped several levels."

CHAPTER TWENTY-EIGHT

Lauren had a great deal on her mind, and a great many decisions to make.

The first order of business was to figure out whether she was safe and if so, where? If Anderson truly had it in for her, how far would and could he go? Was she completely alone in this or who had her back?

She was fairly confident Aaron would watch out for her, no matter what else he had going on in his life. His fate was tied to hers, for the most part. Whether he had a choice in the matter was another thing altogether; Anderson would logically group them together.

The overwhelming question was what had happened to Justin? With all that had been going on, Lauren knew that going to his house could be a fatal mistake. She assumed she was being followed or at least monitored and being tracked in Justin's company without the excuse of the Bartley case was simply too dangerous and unexplainable. She couldn't be attributed to asking too many questions about his

235

whereabouts, even in the office. An attorney should not be concerned with the business of a paralegal and if something were known, she felt sure Betsy would have found a way to get that information to her.

No, it appeared as though Justin had disappeared and she could only pray that he was okay. There was nothing she could do to help him without putting him in even greater danger.

The only course of action Lauren could consider was to go about her life as normal and hope that whatever Anderson was being a prick about, would eventually fade away. Anderson liked challenges and as long as Lauren didn't offer up any new ones, there was a chance the cat would find another mouse to play with.

Lauren went into the office that morning with her normal demeanor. She asked Betsy to set up some appointments to review status on some former cases that had been placed on standby when the Bartley case had been given precedent.

There was no sign of Anderson in the building; apparently he had taken the day off. Aaron was in and out but he stopped by her office and gave her a quiet kiss. It was unspoken between them not to discuss anything at the office where anyone could be listening.

Lauren used the extra time to research Monica's paperwork and discovered exactly what she had expected. She had never cared for Morgan, so this came as no surprise. She debated whether she should even tell Monica.

Secrets. So, so many secrets. She wished with all her heart that she could wipe out any doubts she had; about Aaron, Justin, Morgan...even Anderson. It just didn't seem right that there were so few people she could trust in her life.

She thought about Nikki and how her careless behavior was so very dangerous. Lauren feared she'd get that call someday that Nikki had overdosed or been found stuff in a garbage can. She wondered why Nikki was so cavalier about her reputation. Was she running away from something in her reality? Maybe she and Monica should have a serious sit-down with Nikki and see if they could get through to her. That brought her to Monica, who at this moment had more problems than she could handle.

On an impulse she picked up her phone and tapped Monica's autodial. Monica answered almost immediately.

"Mon, it's me. What are you up to?"

Monica answered in a voice that sounded distant, "I'm shopping apartments."

"Apartments? Why? What's wrong with your house?"

"Morgan is in my house," Monica answered sardonically.

Lauren thought maybe the connection was bad because Monica wasn't making sense.

"You say Morgan is at your house? I don't understand. What's wrong?"

"I left him" came Monica's simple reply.

"You left Morgan?" Lauren was shocked. Morgan may be many things but she knew Monica loved him and that they'd been trying to have a child. This seemed a rash move, even for Monica.

"I'm in the process of it," Monica answered. "He doesn't know yet, so don't say anything." Her voice sounded so matter of fact and Lauren recognized the tone. That meant Monica was deeply hurt and putting on a brave face.

"Mon, let's get together. I'll call Nikki and let's meet at Rinko's. It's about time we had a girls' night out and Nikki has gotten herself into shit again, too. Let's get drunk and clean up messes. You game?"

"Might as well," Monica answered in a resigned voice. "I can't find anyplace decent for my budget so I might have to head out of town."

"Mon, don't do anything just yet, okay? A couple more days won't make any difference and let's get all this sorted out in the meantime. Promise me?" Lauren pleaded.

"Whatever," was Monica's non-committal reply. "When?"

"I'll meet you there tonight at 8. It's a weekend so I can sleep in. I'll call Nikki and unless you hear back from me, just be there, okay?" Lauren wasn't sure she could trust Monica when she was in one of these moods.

"Yeah, okay, see you then," Monica said and the line went dead.

Lauren puzzled over Monica's decision for a few moments before dialing Nikki. She answered in a sleepy voice and at first Lauren wasn't sure if she was sober. Nikki straightened out after a minute and agreed to meet them that night. There was no reference made to the incident at the Marriott and Lauren was actually glad about this. That meant they could put it out in the open when she had Monica there to back her up. Monica wouldn't take Nikki's shit.

"Betsey, take messages, I'm out for the rest of the day," Lauren called over her shoulder as she grabbed her bag and headed out the door. The sunlight felt good on her face and she stood for a few moments, just looking upward and breathing in the fresh air. She texted Aaron that she was going out with the girls and then headed toward her favorite spa to get a massage and her hair done. She decided to get a sassy new haircut; it was time for fresh beginnings.

CHAPTER TWENTY-NINE

Lauren walked in the doors of Rinko's in a very positive mood. She'd gotten a new hairstyle and had stopped to pick up the cutest little dress and heels she'd seen in a store window. She was dressing to give herself a lift in spirits, and to bolster herself for the drama she knew would be coming up with Monica and Nikki.

Rinko's was a popular singles club but the atmosphere and dance music appealed to the young professional set and it was hard to not be infected with the power and ambition that filled its air. It would provide a positive backdrop for their girls' night out.

Monica was already at a table, her feet dangling from the high stool as she watched some dancers on the floor. Lauren slid onto another stool and the waiter timed it with a napkin. Lauren ordered and then hugged Monica. "Hey, girl, how are you?"

Monica didn't look good, in Lauren's opinion. Her eyes were puffy, whether from lack of sleep or crying, but the effect was the same. Her answer was equally lackluster, "You know…" she murmured.

"Mon, cheer up. We'll get through this." Lauren tried to sound supportive and positive but in her gut, she was glad Monica had split from Morgan. Lauren considered him a dead end.

Monica shrugged and sipped her drink, looking out over the dancers in a sort of forlorn, bored manner. Lauren took advantage of the opportunity to tell Monica about the Hilton adventure. Monica's eyebrows raised as the old Mon fired up at Nikki's decadence, but then she seemed to remember herself and retreated back into the bored nonchalance she was choosing to hide behind.

"We need to give her a good talking to, Mon. She can't keep this shit up. She'll end up in a dumpster somewhere," Lauren persuaded.

"We'll talk to her," Monica responded, her voice holding the forecast of brimstone.

Lauren nodded and then saw Nikki making her way toward them between the tables. She was wearing a super mini made of gold lamé and a tank top that barely covered her breasts. She looked at Monica, who had also noticed Nikki and was rolling her eyes. "Lots of talkin'," she added.

Nikki sailed up to them with a huge smile on her face; a smile that suggested she was as innocent as a Spring flower. "Hey, bitches," she offered brightly, undeterred by the glowering looks from Lauren and Monica.

"Hey, Nikki," Lauren returned, hugging her.

Monica was not so gentile. "What the shit are you wearin' girl?" she launched.

Nikki looked down just as the waiter approached, and he looked down as well. "Just something I found in my closet," she popped back and then ordered a drink.

"Like hell," muttered Monica. "You're dressin' for whatever you can take home from here and don't think we don't know that. But you just sit your little ass on that stool and listen to us. This crap has got to stop, Nikki."

Nikki looked at Lauren. "I'm guessing you told her about...." her voice trailed off in expectation.

"You got it," Lauren snapped. "I wasn't going to take this on by myself, but Nikki, do you really think what you're doing gives you any future? Do you want to jump from bed to bed, from drug to drug, your entire life? Don't you want more for yourself than that?"

Monica chose another tact. "Nikki, look bitch, you're gonna end up dead. Now, if that's what you want, tell me now and I'll walk away. I'm not goin' stand by and watch any more curtain calls, because eventually, that audience is goin' to stop clappin'. You get me?"

Nikki was a little surprised at the vehemence of her friends who had always overlooked her little peccadillos. "Hey, don't get all over me. I know what I'm doin'."

Monica snorted. "Like hell you do. I hear that all the time and it's your way of sayin' you don't want to change. You're lucky you're still alive. You just keep slidin' past disaster but the sand is about to run out of your hourglass, girl. I'm not going to speak for Lauren, but I'm not standin' around and watchin'."

Nikki looked out over the dance floor and winked at a dangerous looking guy in a black shirt that was opened down to the navel. Monica snapped, "What's it gonna be lil' girl. Tell me now, 'cause this is a waste of my time."

Nikki didn't answer and finally Lauren elbowed her. "Answer the lady!" she ordered not very politely.

Nikki jerked. "Okay, okay, I get it. I'll clean up my act. I could have done it any time I wanted to. I met a guy anyway…"

Monica rolled her eyes. "What part of meetin' a new guy qualifies as cleanin' up your act?"

"No, no, this one is different. He's one of the good guys," Nikki explained. "He doesn't put up with my shit."

"Well, goooooood for him!" proclaimed Monica. "Who is he?"

Nikki looked Monica in the eye. "I'll tell when I'm ready. Let me make sure he's the one before you start my bridal registry, okay?"

Monica sipped her drink and nodded. "Okay, I'll give you that. But no more shit, Nikki. I hear about one more thing and you can consider me an ex-friend. Got it?"

Nikki nodded and looked back over the dance floor. She had a sort of blank look on her face and was very thoughtful.

Lauren let out a sigh, glad that the confrontation was over. She could relax now and emptied her glass while signaling to the waiter to bring another.

She looked out to the dance floor, tapping the table to the rhythm. Maybe she could catch somebody's eye and he'd come ask her to dance. Her new hair and outfit were going to waste at this table.

That's when she saw him. Her mouth dropped open and her heart plummeted.

On the far side of the floor danced Justin...and he was not alone. There was a gorgeous blonde dancing

246

across from him and they were laughing, obviously well acquainted with one another.

Lauren felt the blood drain from her head and thought she might faint. *Why is he here and who is the blonde? At least I know he's safe. Did he abandon me? Is that where Anderson got all his information? Could he have had something to do with Bartley's suicide?* The questions flooded her brain, making her dizzy and instantly anxious. She wanted to leave before he saw her, but somehow her legs were blocks and wouldn't move from the stool.

There was a voice at her elbow and she turned to see a tall, good-looking man with his hand out, offering her to dance. Lauren hesitated and looked back toward Justin. With resolve, she finally nodded and smiled at the stranger, taking the outstretched hand and heading out to the dance floor.

Just then the music changed and a slow song began. The stranger shrugged and held out his arm. Lauren took it. The couples floated around the floor and Lauren kept her eyes focused on her partner.

247

The song was almost finished when she looked up and dancing right next to them was Justin...and his eyes were locked on hers.

CHAPTER THIRTY

Lauren could barely breathe. Justin was staring at her face to see her expression. Not knowing what to think or do, she chose to politely nod.

Justin's face fell and she could see he was confused. Her heart broke to be so cold, but she had no idea what she was dealing with and couldn't afford to reveal anything here in public, particularly with Nikki and Monica watching.

The stranger she was dancing with was speaking. "So, little lady, what are you doing when you leave here tonight?" he was grinning.

Lauren shuddered and dropped her hands. "You know... I'm feeling a little ill just now. The dancing is making my head swim, I think I'd better sit down for a while," she said and turned to go back to the table where Monica and Nikki waited. The stranger stood there, abandoned on the dance floor with a stunned look on his face. He figured he had hit the jackpot.

"Jesus!" Monica exclaimed as Lauren sat down. "What was that all about?"

Lauren turned her face to stone. "He was a creep, made a pass and I headed for the bench," she said curtly but this left Monica and Nikki puzzled since Lauren was always so composed. Clearly she was upset about something.

"Okaaaaaaay, if you say so," Nikki responded, rolling her eyes at Monica, who nodded.

The music changed and Lauren ordered another drink. She had the curious urge to get very drunk. She had no idea who the woman with Justin was, but they looked pretty friendly. Lauren instantly despised her. She got restless and decided to get her own drink. Leaving the stool, she headed for the bar.

The bartender took her order and she chose a stool to wait. That put the dance floor at her back, which was exactly where she wanted it to be. It was busy and the drink was slow in coming. There was an arm on her elbow and she swiveled to find Justin standing there.

"Lauren." His voice was a simple statement.

"Justin," she acknowledged cooly.

"What's wrong?" he asked.

"Really? You really have to ask?" she said in a voice filled with sarcasm.

"You look beautiful tonight," he whispered.

"Justin. Stop. I can't be seen talking to you and really don't know why I even should. You have simply disappeared and left me to face the wolves alone. Now, here you are with a bitch in tow."

She received her drink, nodded to the bartender to put it on her tab and swiveled away from Justin to leave. He caught her elbow and said into her ear, "Lauren, don't be ridiculous. You don't know the story and the woman is no one for you to worry about."

"Who said I was worried, Justin? I'm a married woman, you know."

"I know," he said darkly. "You don't have to remind me."

"Good!" she popped back and spun out of his grasp, heading for the table with the girls.

"What's wrong with you?" Monica asked when she returned. "You're pissed."

"No, I'm not."

"Girl, it's all over your face and in the way you swung your ass on the way back to the table. I know that walk – have done it a few times myself."

"Never mind, it's nothing. The bartender made a pass."

"Well, lucky you, he's cute," murmured Nikki.

"Forget it Nikki," Monica warned.

"I know, I know…" Nikki's voice trailed off with longing.

Lauren was simply relieved that the conversation had turned away from her so she said nothing more. They continued to sip drinks and talk about gossip.

Some time later the waiter approached with a fresh round of drinks. Puzzled, the women looked at him.

"Compliments of a mystery man he told me to say," the waiter filled in.

Monica frowned, Nikki smiled and Lauren felt her face flush. She knew *exactly* who had sent them.

Just as the waiter turned to leave, he slipped a small piece of paper into Lauren's hand. She felt it and knew enough to not react. He moved away.

Lauren was watching the dance floor. Pointing at a man in a particularly tight pair of pants, she mentioned that she thought he had a cute butt. Monica and Nikki automatically followed her finger and their gazes lingered. Lauren took advantage of the diversion to read the note.

Come to the ladies room at the back of the bar.

She knew the handwriting in an instant. *What on earth is he up to?* she wondered. She slipped the note into her waistband and laughed as Monica and Nikki both were straining to see the guy's butt. Nikki was running her hand against the back of her neck; a sign that she was getting ready to pounce on someone.

Monica saw it as well and nodded to Lauren. "C'mon, Nikki, let's go pee."

Lauren froze. Whatever Justin was up to, it didn't include an open invitation to the others, she was sure of that. She didn't even know if she was willing to see him herself.

Nikki was looking at her. "What's that?" she asked.

"I said aren't you coming with us?" Nikki answered.

"No, you go on ahead. I'll stay and watch purses," Lauren improvised. Nikki nodded and they headed to the bathroom at the front of the club, Lauren noticed with relief.

While they were gone she swung around and looked toward the ladies room door at the back of the bar. There was no sign of Justin anywhere. Was she wrong? Could it have been someone else? Who? The sleezy guy she had danced with? No, he was too simple-minded for something that subtle.

She scanned the dance floor and then the tables. Justin was nowhere to be seen. However, his date, was.

She was walking back into the interior of the club from the direction of the entrance and a very handsome man was in tow. She stopped twice to kiss him passionately and he slid his hand possessively over her ass. *Odd* Lauren thought to herself. *Why would Justin's date be making out with another man, right out in the open?*

About then, Monica and Nikki slid back onto their stools. "Whew!" Monica explained. "Someone puked in there and no one bothered to clean it up. I 'bout lost it myself!"

Lauren wrinkled her nose. "Naturally, as soon as you two left, I felt the need, but I believe I'll choose another powder room," she improvised. Monica nodded and Nikki was panning the dance floor for the cute ass.

Lauren picked up her bag and headed for the back ladies room. She had just pushed the door open when a hand grabbed her and the lights went dark. She opened her mouth to scream, but a large hand was planted firmly over her. The door was pushed shut and she distinctly heard the click of a lock.

CHAPTER THIRTY-ONE

Lauren froze in terror until the hand lowered and a pair of warm lips that were instantly recognizable were searching her own.

"Hold still, darling, it's me. There was no other way to see you. I've bribed the manager to hang an *Out of Service* sign on the door and we have this to ourselves for the next fifteen minutes."

Lauren started laughing, "Who are you? James Bond? You lure me into a women's bathroom?"

"Can you think of anywhere less liable to be discovered?"

"True," Lauren chuckled again. Then she was instantly sober. "Who is the woman?"

"What woman?" Justin was puzzled.

"Don't be coy with me, Justin. She was all over you."

"If you mean Janice, she wasn't over anything on me, darlin'. She's a childhood friend and I was doing her husband a favor by keeping her escorted until he arrived."

Lauren considered this and felt guilty for not having trusted him. She had, indeed, seen the woman leading another man by the hand just before Justin's note had reached her.

"Sorry, but you can't blame me. You disappeared and left me to deal with Anderson and this entire mess on my own!"

Justin was silent a moment and then flipped on the light. There was a puzzled look on his face. "You didn't know?"

Lauren stared at him. "Know what?"

"Damn!" he cursed. "Fuck Anderson!"

"What?" Lauren asked, reaching with her hand to cup his cheek. "What is it?"

Justin slammed his fist into the wall, causing the mirrors above the sinks to tilt. "Fuckin' Anderson swore to me he would let you know."

"Know what?" Lauren asked, trying to piece together what Justin was talking about.

Justin swung toward Lauren and suddenly picked her up by the waist and swung her to sit on the counter. He put one hand on either side of her so she was forced to look closely into his face and could not look away.

"I want you to listen to me very carefully, this is important," Justin began. Lauren nodded, eyes wide and puzzled. "Anderson called me at home. He told me that Bartley's body had been found and that things were going to explode. He said he knew about you and I and that unless I wanted it all to come out, and your reputation to be ruined, I should stay out of the office."

Lauren opened her mouth to ask a question, but Justin quickly shook his head and kept talking. "I didn't want to leave you to the hounds, but there was nothing I could do at the moment that would be safer for you than to stay away. Nothing, Lauren, you have to believe me."

Lauren nodded.

"He told me that he would explain it to you privately so you wouldn't worry and that he didn't give a shit what you and I did down the line, but right now there would be enough uproar over Bartley to topple the firm's reliability image and if you and I surfaced, there was no way he could control it. So, I did as promised. I stayed away, no messages, no computer access, nothing. I didn't even text you because I was sure the phones were bugged. I did it for you, darlin'...not for the firm and certainly not for Anderson."

Lauren nodded and threw her arms around his neck, relief flooding her entire body. She felt guilty for having damned him without evidence. If anyone, as a lawyer she should have known not to pronounce guilt until all the evidence was in. In this case, none of the evidence, except Justin's absence, was available.

Justin's mouth came down on hers and the hunger was overwhelming. Their mouths could not seem to

259

get close enough. His tongue probed her, encircling her tongue and then sucking at it with such a force that it almost hurt. She bit his bottom lip and then quickly kissed it, running her tongue to trace the outside of his lips.

Justin's mouth travelled down to her neck, licking and gently biting. Her tongue went into his ear and explored each crevice, blowing cool air to alternate with the moist heat of her tongue. The effect was electric shocks that ran through the length of him.

His hands found her hemline and he whipped the dress off over her head in one smooth move. She was still reeling from their kisses and barely noticed and it wasn't until he had removed her thong that the cool draft made her aware.

In turn she tore at his shirt, yanking it up over his head so that she could press her skin against his chest. Her nipples responded to his heat and the soft hairs across his broad torso. She heard Justin groan and immediately his mouth was feeding upon her nipples, sucking and licking, the moan of need and desire emanating from deep within his throat.

Suddenly Justin stiffened and stood straight. He took her face into his hands and said in a husky, raw voice, "I love you, Lauren. I *will* have you, you belong to me."

Lauren's eyes filled with tears of joy and she felt his hands on her woman's nest. She groaned with the sensation and desperate need she'd felt for so many weeks.

Her legs parted wider and she threw one leg over each of his shoulders. He groaned at the scent of her and latched on to her pussy with his mouth, sucking her pubic lips deeply into his mouth. Lauren lay backward, driving herself upward and into his mouth while his hands grasped her ass and he inserted his finger inside. Lauren screamed at the invasion but it crazed her; she rocked back and forth, trying to get more deeply into his mouth and to impale herself upon his finger.

Just as he was about to thrust his throbbing hardness, into her, she pushed his hands aside and slid down onto the pile of clothes on the floor, pulling him with her. Justin complied and watched with fascination as Lauren straddled his chest while facing his dick.

She wriggled slowly and tantalizingly closer and closer to his face and finally he could stand no more; he pulled her down to cover his face and drilled her with his tongue. Lauren, driven to frenzy by the fire, lay flat and took his rigid penis into her mouth, pushing it as far into her throat as she could.

Justin groaned at the suction she applied, her fingers working his balls and the tender skin just beneath. She slid a long fingernail into the crack of his ass and skimmed the tender skin until she, too, could push more deeply inside. The made Justin frantic and he threw her over in a wrestler's move and loomed above her that critical moment before he drove inside her. She could feel herself flood and the soft flesh of her clit closed around him, sucking him deeply inside.

Lauren's head fell backward, exposing her lovely throat to his lips. Justin felt suddenly bereft because he could not touch every inch of her with himself at that moment. He plunged into her and her cries of delight impassioned him further.

Each was aware of only one another, and yet of the clock ticking. Each sensed this might be the beginning of an end between them, and yet neither willed it to be so. With each stroke Justin claimed what was his, and Lauren surrendered herself, her soul being sucked into his at their very core. She knew she would never be alone, no matter where she went; Justin would be inside her.

She felt tears spilling down her cheeks; the burning joy of having Justin buried within her contrasting with the knowledge that in simply moments...it would end.

They exploded at the same time because Justin held out until he knew she was ready. They shared that moment, that golden starburst of knowing you are loved and time is perfect. Neither heard the music from the dance floor, the people talking, or the clinks of glasses. For them, in that moment, only they existed.

Lauren's legs still wrapped around his waist, Justin lowered her once again to the counter. With sadness and regret he retrieved their clothing. Lauren tossed her panties into the trash, as they were useless.

She reached down with a finger into herself, coating it with their juices and then traced Justin's lips. "This is us, my darling," she said softly. "Remember how we are and how this is between us. Remember that I love you, Justin, no matter what may happen to pull us apart."

"We won't be apart," he growled. "You belong to me, you were supposed to be mine from the start. I won't let you go." His eyes looked as though he would cry, huge and desperate with wanting to keep her at his side.

She nodded slowly and whispered, "I know...I know..." There was a discrete knock at the door then and she quickly slid down to the floor, her legs wobbling from the exertion and contrast to supporting her own, love-sodden weight. "I love you, Justin."

He kissed her again, long and hard. "You're mine, Lauren. Never forget that," he whispered and then went to the door. Flipping off the light so as not to attract attention, he unlocked the door and slid out, his hand flipping the light back on as the door gently closed.

Lauren was shaking and she went to the sink and bathed her heated face, raw from Justin's slight stubble and the pressure of their lovemaking. She looked at herself in the mirror and quickly searched for a comb. There was no way the girls wouldn't see it all over her.

She left the bathroom and sailed to the table. "I don't feel well, too much to drink. I'm out of here," was all she said, grabbing her wrap and leaving Monica and Nikki staring at her retreating figure as she headed for the door and the cool night air outside.

She found her car and once inside, locked the door as if she could lock out the stale, dirty world that could wipe away the aura of Justin's lovemaking upon her. She sat for a very long time with her eyes closed, her head reclined against the headrest, doing her best to inscribe the memory of what had just happened deeply onto her brain. She wanted to be able to recall it at will in the days ahead. She sensed that she would need that. That was when the tears began and soon her shoulders quaked with sobbing. Her heart no longer belonged to her and this sensation terrified her. She felt out of control with passion and longing for someone she could not have. Even his words...that she belonged to him...threatened to choke her because she knew that may never be.

Lauren drove home that night, in the aftermath of passion, but with a hatred for the entire world.

CHAPTER THIRTY-TWO

Aaron stood before the elevator, watching the numbers click downward as it came to meet him. He dreaded this encounter; knowing that his entire life was about to change. This was something he did not want to do, had never imagined himself in this position, but he knew there was no turning back.

This isn't fair to Lauren, he thought to himself. He felt guilt for shutting her out; it was a betrayal and there was no other word to describe it.

The elevator doors opened to admit him then, and Aaron stepped inside, bound for Hell.

Nikki stared at her reflection in the mirror. This was something she generally did when creating the face the world would see. Her makeup table was covered with Plexiglas racks, filled with powders, creams and tiny tubes and vials of rainbow colors. Her face lived in those expensive little containers.

Now, however, she confronted herself, void of color and the masks they provided. She saw her eyes and noted that there were tiny crows feet beginning to crease the tender skin at the corners. *That's from the dope and the smokes* she thought to herself and reached for a jar of cream, but then stopped.

She looked at the prized hair and saw that it no longer glowed as it once did. *Too many sleepless nights* she thought again.

Her breasts were perky but she knew that was simply a matter of time. Everything about her reeked of a ticking clock and excess, the sort from which one eventually cannot recover. Nikki grimaced; her carefree days were numbered.

She did not want to die alone. Sometimes that was what entered her head when she snorted a line while in the company of her latest amore. *At least I wouldn't die alone* she would think, tempted to take more than she should. *What does that say about me?* she asked herself. She did not want to end up in a black body bag, wheeled like a shrunken queen on a gurney to the waiting ambulance and her hole in the ground. She wanted more from life than that; in fact she wanted children.

Would I make a good mother? she wondered. Then she would begin to think of having a little girl...of having a miniature of herself; someone to dress and curl hair, someone to take to ballet lessons and teach to play the piano. The thought of this made her feel very good, very satisfied. Perhaps that's what she was meant to do at this point in her life.

Encouraged by this, she applied the cream to the edges of her eyes, but now with the attitude of preservation, not disguise. She finished her hair and let it lie naturally, instead of using products to make it stand on end. She dropped the vivid red lipsticks into the trash, as well as the peacock blues and purple eye shadows. Instead she picked up the soft pink and the effect startled her...she looked like her mother!

Suddenly she knew without a doubt the motivation for her behavior. She hated her mother; that sadistic, selfish bitch who made her sit in the living room when she entertained men. Nikki knew then that as long as she rode the wild card, she was throwing the dice. Maybe she wouldn't live long enough to have children, maybe she didn't deserve to have children. Maybe she belonged in that black bag, just like her mother had worn when the needle stuck in her arm. Her mother had taken the easy way out when the men stopped coming around. Nikki didn't want to be alone, but not because she feared death...she feared life.

CHAPTER THIRTY-THREE

Justin had become a fever. Lauren thought of no one else and even her work had grown mundane and repetitive in the glow of remembering his mouth and his hands. She chided herself, knowing she was feeling the rush that new romance always carried with it. But this was different somehow...the stakes were higher.

She was a married woman and no matter what, or who, Aaron was up to, she had an innate respect for the law, and adultery was a coat she did not wear well. She felt as though she was the ultimate hypocrite; faithful in theory but not in body.

She tried to convince herself that Aaron was being unfaithful and that gave her the green light to behave likewise. Perhaps they would forever be one of those couples that had an "understanding." She had to ask herself if she could be content with that.

Even though Justin gave her flutters and made her wet, did she want him to be the one and only for the rest of her life? Was she even cut out to be a one and only type of woman? She had spent her life breaking the glass ceiling, investing everything she had, and was, into becoming respected in a man's world. Would restricting herself to one man, one husband, be enough? Was she damned to be on some eternal quest for superiority? Perhaps she should visit a shrink, but knew instantly that she already possessed any answers that were available.

At the moment, all she could think about, however, was Justin. It was as if a warm, sweet juice poured through her mind and into her depths; she need only remember his mouth upon her in their bathroom tryst to prime the juices over and over again. Sometimes it was so overwhelming that she pulled her car over to a parking lot just so she could shut her eyes and relive the sensations he had brought to her surface.

What made it so luxurious was the idea that only Justin and she knew what lay between them. She could never tell Monica or Nikki; it could potentially destroy their friendship. Lauren had always been a sort of icon of success to them; they depended on her for wisdom and to be a stabilizer in their haphazard trio. If they knew what she was up to, the three of them would fall apart.

Lauren had decided to take a few days off and do a bit of redecorating. Even though they could easily afford a decorator, she enjoyed the creative outlet and looked forward to changing the colors in her bedroom. She was ready for a new start.

She was paging through a Laura Ashley design book when her cell buzzed. It was Justin.

"I thought you weren't going to call me?" she said as soon as she picked up the phone.

"Can't help it. Meet me?" he asked simply.

Lauren hesitated; she was in jeans and one of Aaron's old shirts, preparing to clean closets. "It will take me a bit to be ready," she began.

"Come as you are, it's important. You know where I am," he said in a hurried voice. "Come now," he added urgently.

"On my way," she responded and laid the phone down. She ran upstairs to at least change shirts and throw on some lipstick, grabbing her bag and a rain slicker as she headed downstairs.

273

Aaron was standing in the living room. "Oh!" she said, startled. "I didn't know you were home," she said breathlessly.

"I guess you weren't expecting me?" Aaron countered, an odd look on his face. "I tried calling but it went straight to voice mail," he added.

That explains the beeping when I was talking to Justin she thought to herself.

"I'm just on my way out," she began, scrambling for a reason before he asked.

"So I see," he said, pointing at the slicker she held in her hand. "Want some company?"

Lauren flushed, slid on the coat to cut this scene short and quickly said, "No, it's okay. I'm going to shop for some bedding and sort of enjoy doing that alone," she covered. Smiling, she tossed her bag up over her shoulder and turned toward the door. As she turned the knob Aaron called to her.

"Did you forget something?" he asked and Lauren turned back, thinking he wanted a kiss goodbye. Instead he held out her cell phone in his open hand.

"Oh, yeah," she laughed nervously and reached for the phone. Its face was still lit and the caller ID with Justin's name was blatantly still on the display. Lauren flushed with guilt and looked up at Aaron who simply stood there, a passive, but secretive look upon his face. *Perhaps it's his way of giving me permission* she thought to herself. "I'll see you later," she threw over her shoulder.

"Lauren?" His voice rang like the deepest bell in the church tower. She turned slowly, not sure what to be prepared for. "Be careful, darling," he said softly. It was really difficult to discern the look on his face. Was he being sincere, or was he warning her?

Only time would tell.

Lauren arrived at Justin's house and he let her in the door and immediately threw his arms around her. She melted and it took little effort for him to pick her up and swing her down on the sofa. He peeled off her clothing and suckled upon every part of her body before thrusting himself deeply inside. They both uttered a cry that was more of a sigh of relief. It was a coming together that each needed, more than breath. Later, he lay upon her, keeping her warm with the heat of his body. "I thought you'd never get here," he whispered.

She nodded and then asked, "What's wrong? Why did you call me?"

"I wanted you," he said simply.

She pushed him backward and looked into his face. "Justin, we can't do this. We'll get caught and no one, absolutely no one will benefit from that right now."

He stood and began pulling his pants on. "Darlin', I'm not that stupid. Of course, there's more. I got a call from Anderson this morning," he said, zipping up.

"Oh?" Lauren responded, pulling on her shirt.

Justin turned and saw her sitting there on his sofa, a half-buttoned shirt covering nothing and her womanhood openly displayed upon his cushions. It occurred to him that he would love to have a picture of her, just as she looked in that moment. He would inscribe it on his brain and remember her that way always.

He released a breath of renewed desire and scrambled for clear thought. "He told me not to show up for another week. He wasn't asking," he said.

"What do you suppose he's up to?" Lauren asked, clutching the shirt in a gesture of self-protection.

"I don't know, but you need to know this isn't done yet," Justin said, coming over to sit next to her, his fingertip running down the opening of her shirt and circling her nipples before sliding down to her crotch.

"Justin, I'm serious now," Lauren protested weakly.

"Oh, I am, too," he said, sliding his finger into her tenderness. Lauren groaned, her desire was immediately lit.

"Justin, don't." She pushed away his hand. "We need to talk. I miss you and there's no good reason for you to stay away," she said.

"There's one very good reason, and his name is Anderson," Justin countered. "Lauren, I'm not sure

277

what he's up to, but we can't risk pissing him off any more than he already is. We can't get in his way...it's not worth it."

"Justin, I'm not scared of Anderson," she returned, buttoning up her blouse.

"You should be and you had better be," Justin said. "Seriously, Lauren," he stood up and went to the window. "Anderson is dangerous and not just because he's connected," Justin said. He turned away from the window and faced her. "He's dangerous because he thinks he's right. People are always dangerous in righteousness," he added.

She looked past him, out the window. She saw the reflection of a man in her car window, but before she could call attention to it, it was gone. *Must be my imagination* she told herself.

"I'll be careful," she promised, but wondered just how much she could control.

CHAPTER THIRTY-FOUR

Monica had been raised in a small town in the mid-South. There were no doctors for fifty miles around and so her mother, a trained nurse, looked after many of the local people, including acting as mid-wife. Monica had often accompanied her mother to look in on patients and was no stranger to the coming and going of human life. She had once considered becoming a nurse herself, but then moved to the east coast where doctors were more plentiful and nurses less trusted.

Thus, it came to be that when Morgan's father was diagnosed with acute diabetes and failing kidneys that she would step in and become his caregiver. Three times each week she drove to his tiny house on Tucker Street and transported him to the dialysis clinic. While he was connected to the machine, she would drive back to his house to clean, make dinners and portion them out for freezing and in general, make sure his life was as good as it could be under the circumstances.

When doctors' appointments came up, she could be depended upon to take him and sit in on the consultation so she could ask the right questions and coordinate his care.

Julius Hammond was a proud man and had considerable integrity. Monica was the only person he trusted completely and they had formed a strong bond. She had always hoped that Morgan would see his father as an example to follow and she and Julius discussed Morgan's wayward inclinations often. In many ways she felt closer to Julius than Morgan; perhaps because there were no secrets between them. The same could not be said for Morgan and she, and this saddened her even more.

She had hoped that a baby might make the difference; give them something they shared forever through life and spur Morgan to become more responsible. She knew this was foolish; that a baby should not be brought into an unstable situation out of fairness to the child. Julius, too, wanted to see a grandchild before his days were done and she felt a certain responsibility to give him that one precious wish.

Now life had conspired to separate her from Morgan, but she could not tell Julius this. She knew he could not withstand the blow of that reality and would give up on life entirely. In some sense, she felt it her responsibility to keep up the pretense of happiness. It would cost her some, but it would cost Julius far more if he knew the truth.

It was Monday, and Julius' day for dialysis. She guided her car down Tucker Street and found him waiting for her on his front porch. He had a pair of rockers in its shade and she and Julius often rocked and shared iced tea and long conversations. The realization that she wouldn't always have this retreat hit her then and her eyes teared up. She had imagined holding a baby while she rocked next to Julius, and that he would patiently wait while she fed the child so he could hold it once again and tell it stories from his past.

If she left, would Morgan step in and take care of his father? She doubted it; Morgan was not the caretaking type. He would be more likely to put Julius into a nursing home somewhere, to get haphazard care that would finish him. She couldn't let that happen and resolved to be in Julius' life, no matter what. So, for now, she would play a role...the game. She would pretend that all was at peace between she and Morgan and in that way, keep Julius' whole and happy during whatever time he had left on earth.

She was, after all, her mother's daughter.

Julius stood and started down the porch stairs but she quickly jumped out and supported his elbow to make sure he didn't fall. She had to do this tenderly because his arms were both blackened and tender from the many dialysis insertions of tubes. He always looked bloated from the drugs they gave him and carried a small satchel with a chocolate candy bar and insulin. Julius was, what was often called, "brittle" in that his sugar could drop and escalate very quickly. These were necessities to keep his sugar as level as possible.

"Hello baby doll," he said to her, using the nickname he had given her when she and Morgan had married.

"How ya' feelin', Julius?" she cooed back in that voice she reserved only for him.

282

"Another day, another dime," he'd say, alluding to the money the dialysis clinic was making each time he came in to buy a bit more life.

"Now, Julius, you know you're lucky they're this close to you. It could be worse; we could have to drive all afternoon to get there," she answered softly.

"I don't as that would be such a horrible thing, baby doll," he said, chuckling. "I can think of few people I'd rather spend an afternoon with," he added, winking at her.

She loved him, this crumpled man who walked bravely despite the pain she knew he was feeling. He had already required amputation of his left little toe from the diabetes and it caused him to often stumble. He never complained, though, and this only made him more of a hero in her eyes.

"You'd better quit flirting with me, you know," she said, teasing. "I might just decide I like older men!"

He laughed outright at this, gripping the car door as she helped to lower him inside. "It's about time you figured out I'm flirting," he countered and she could

283

hear him cackle softly as she rounded the back of the car before getting in the driver's seat.

She drove him to the clinic and helped to get him settled before returning to Tucker Street to begin cleaning. She was stripping the bed to wash the sheets when a shadow blocked the light in the doorway. Startled, Monica swung around to find Morgan standing there.

He was smiling. "How are you babe?" he asked in a cheerful voice.

She stopped and as she faced him said, "That's not a term I want to hear from you again, considering the circumstances."

A frown fell upon his brow but he recovered quickly, having had so much practice, and smiled, "I don't blame you, Mon. I know I've been a bastard," he offered.

"Hmph!" was all she offered and turned to finish stripping the sheets. She gathered them in an armload and headed to the doorway. "Let me by, please," she said, waiting for him to stand back. Instead, Morgan leaned forward and took the sheets from her arms, and then proceeded to the back porch where the washing machine waited. She followed and after he deposited the fabric, she added detergent and bleach and tapped the regular cycle button as she lowered the lid.

She was about to turn away when Morgan's arms encircled her from behind, his hands cupping her breasts. He pulled her back against his chest and whispered into her ear. "I miss you, Mon. Come home to me."

At first she melted against his chest, the comfort of his arms over-riding the memory of what he had done to her. "No," she said finally. "I can't do that."

Instead of arguing with her, Morgan nodded, his chin tapping the top of her head. "I understand," he said softly. "But I'm not giving up, and neither should you," he added. Monica stood there a few moments longer and then pushed his arms down before heading into the kitchen and running water into the sink for dishes.

"Mon?" Morgan said from the doorway to the back porch.

"Yeah?" was her soft response.

"Thank you. For Julius, I mean... It would kill him to know we're apart." Morgan's voice actually sounded compassionate and for a moment, she clung to that sound because it meant emotion she wasn't sure he was capable of.

"Sure," she answered. "He's my dad, too, you know," she added, shutting off the faucet and picking up a dishcloth.

"In many ways, you're more family to him than I could ever be," Morgan said generously. Monica nodded without looking around and the next sound she heard was Morgan leaving through the back screen door.

She stood at the sink, tears sliding into the hot dishwater. They were tears of disappointment, of regret and of dubious hope...but they were tears that meant her heart had not yet let go.

CHAPTER THIRTY-FIVE

Her hand was shaking a bit as she hit the keypad on the phone. It had been days since she'd had a drink and her body was giving her hell for it. She took a deep inhale of the cigarette in her hand; there were, after all, limits to this self-improvement kick and she was giving herself credit for how far she'd come.

Nikki cleared her raspy throat as her finger hovered over the "Send" button.

"Hello?"

"Hi, this is Nikki. Remember me?" she tried not to sound too needy, but at the moment, that was exactly how she felt.

"Of course. How are you?"

"Well, that's just the thing. Not so great."

"Oh, what's wrong? Can I help?"

Nikki hesitated a moment and then said, "Yes, I believe you are exactly the only person at this moment who can help. Would you have time to come by?"

"I'm on my way." The line went silent and Nikki set the phone down, her hand shaking. She was setting off on a new path now and had no idea if she would like it.

There came a knock at the door. Sighing at the feeling of her commitment, Nikki got up from the paisley sofa and the emerald knitted throw and went to answer it. She was wearing a pair of skinny jeans and an oversized sweater; the combination seemed to suit her mood.

"Hello," she said as she opened the door.

"Nikki, are you okay?" Brad asked.

"I am now that you're here," she whispered and then burst into tears.

Brad was alarmed. He didn't think Nikki was the type to cry and there must be something really upsetting her. "What is it? What's wrong?" he asked and led her to the sofa.

Nikki didn't answer, but buried her face into the warmth of his chest and although Brad found this very pleasing, he was concerned why the Nikki he had been with was so very different from the woman sprawled over him now. He let her cry until there was nothing left but shuddering breaths.

Brad took her chin in his hand and lifted her face to look at him. "Now, you want to tell me what's going on?"

Nikki's eyes were like glass paperweights; full of tears with a beautiful iris glistening beneath. "I'm going straight," she said with finality.

Brad tried not to laugh because he could tell that she was very, very serious about what she was saying. He knew if even cracked a smile, it would devastate her.

"Suppose you explain what you mean by that," he coaxed and Nikki's breath sobbed inward again.

Nikki drew a tissue out of her pocket and sat back, holding his hand in one of hers. She began. "I've been wild all my life, you know..." she started and Brad nodded with full sincerity. "It's like I've been ridden by a devil. I never gave a shit about my reputation, told 'em to fuck themselves. It's none of anybody's business how I run my life." Again Brad nodded solemnly in agreement. "But where has it gotten me? You know? I'm all fucked up. I've only got a couple of friends and the rest of the people I've known are like some fucking conga line of motherfuckers who fucked me. Sorry for the "fucks" but you'll see my point in a minute.

Nikki's tissue was now a round ball of snot and she lifted the edge of her sweater to wipe her nose, but Brad leapt up and retrieved some paper towel from the kitchen counter. "Here, use this," he offered. "You don't have to wear it afterwards," he added, trying to add some levity to the situation.

"See what I mean?" she said. "I can't even blow my fucking nose right!"

"You're fine, you're fine, keep going," he encouraged.

Nikki sniffed loudly and said, "I've been trying to figure out why I'm so fucked up. Shrinks can't help me; they don't know what the fuck they're doin'. They're all nuts themselves, anyway. You know?"

Brad nodded in agreement again.

"So, I had a long talk with myself and I started bringing back some memories from when I was a kid. My mom was a whore, did you know that?" she looked up at Brad for confirmation. He shook his head. "Well, she was," Nikki went on. "And a damned good one, too. Made lots of bucks. But she always said she didn't want me to do like her. I used to think it was because she was trying to protect me, but now I realized she just didn't want her daughter as competition, doing tricks and stealing hers."

Brad stiffened a bit but feigned a shift in seating to hide his reaction. "I didn't know," he said.

Nikki nodded. "Anyway, the whole kid thing was fucked up in every way possible and there's only so much of that you can take and still see the world as not one giant fucked up piece of shit. So, I've lived like shit because it seemed the best way to survive."

Brad hesitated to ask any questions while she was on a roll. "It's okay, Nikki. Anyone would be fucked up by that," he said, hoping it sounded encouraging. He could tell she needed to bleed the wound in order to feel better.

"Brad, you're the only one who ever treated me decent," she said. "You and I were only together a couple of times, but you were so different. You made me feel like a lady, like I was worth something."

"You are worth something; a great deal of something," he said encouragingly.

"I'm done fucking around," she said with finality. "And just to show you, I'm going to quit using the word "fuck.""

Brad smile very mildly and said, "That sounds like a good start," and Nikki's eyes flashed until she realized he was being supportive and teasing her, and then she relaxed again.

"Will you help me?" Nikki asked.

"Not say fuck?" Brad teased.

"You know what I mean, asshole!" she flashed. "Will you help me bury the old Nikki in some crap can in the bay and help me be more of the woman you treated me to be?"

Brad took her chin once again and looked her straight in the eyes. "It would be my supreme pleasure," he said in the most loving voice she could ever imagine and she melted. "Let's begin by you going in there and putting on a dress and I'll take you to dinner at a swanky place. What do you say?"

Nikki managed a smile and nodded, scampering up off the sofa to change her clothes.

"And Nikki," he said from the sofa.

"Yeah?" she answered, turning on her pretty heel.

"Make sure your ass isn't hanging out, will you?" Brad said with a glint in his eyes.

"You bastard!" Nikki snapped and instantly closer her mouth when he held an admonishing finger up

293

toward her. "This is going to be hard," she said, shaking her head. "Very, very hard."

Brad just smiled. He was very…very happy.

CHAPTER THIRTY-SIX

Lauren strode into her office with all the authority and confidence she could muster. She knew she was in enemy territory and it wouldn't do to show weakness. Betsey followed her in and had a timid look on her face. "Mr. Anderson wishes to see you as soon as you come in," she said hesitantly.

Lauren could feel the anxiety hit her stomach, but swallowed and said in a brave voice, "I'll be right in." She picked up her tablet and headed toward Anderson's lair.

Tapping on the door, she entered without waiting for acknowledgement; a show of strength on her part. "Mr. Anderson? You wanted to confer with me?" She was using her best-dressed language.

Anderson looked up from his desk. "Come in, Lauren. Take a seat." There was no way to hear anything but a threat and danger in his voice, but Lauren did as she was bid.

"How can I help you?" she began the discussion, hoping to set the tone with her own authority.

"I'll come right to the point," he shut her down. "There's going to be an investigation by the Attorney General's office into Bartley's death."

Lauren was puzzled. "Why? Wasn't it a suicide?"

"Of course it was!" he blurted, somewhat too vehemently for what should be a given fact.

"Then why?" she began.

"You will have to ask them that, counselor, but I'm here to tell you that you know nothing, do you understand?"

Lauren shrank a bit at his tone. *Why was he getting so upset? Why is he on the defensive?* she asked herself. She looked at him with a quizzical look on her face. "Ohhhhhkay.... is there something I should know?" she ventured.

"Exactly my point, Mrs. Reynolds, there is absolutely *nothing* you should know, nor venture a guess about. Are we understood?"

Lauren nodded and stood, hesitated a moment but Anderson looked back down at his desk so she left the room, but her curiosity was definitely piqued.

Lauren found Betsy at the water cooler and motioned her into the office. Betsy's brown eyes were huge as she came in to the room and closed the glass door. "Is everything okay?" she ventured.

Lauren smiled, "For the moment, it's fine. For the future, it might be even better. I want you to do something for me, but keep it on the quiet. No one, and I stress *no one* in the office is to know you are doing this. I want you to find out everything you can about the death of our client, Bartley. Start with the papers, the Internet, coroner's records, anything at all. Extend your search to anyone who would be considered his friend or close associate, and naturally, anyone in his family, living and dead. Got it?"

Betsy nodded. "Would it help if I knew what I was looking for?"

Lauren looked up, her face solemn. "No, it would not. Just bring it all to me. Let me look it over and decide what is and what isn't important. Everything,

Betsy, and keep it off the office computers. I want no paper trail. Got it?" Lauren finished.

Betsy nodded, her eyes huge.

"I mean it, Betsy, not a word." Lauren warned again.

Betsy nodded and turned to leave.

"Betsy?" Lauren said in a less tense voice.

"Yes?"

"Thank you," Lauren offered gently. "It's important or I wouldn't ask you to do this or put you in this position. I can't do this personally for reasons I will explain at some point in the future."

"I know, it's okay. I'll do my best," Betsy smiled encouragingly.

LAUREN: Can you meet me now?

JUSTIN: I'll be waiting.

Lauren pulled into the drive and Justin was already standing in the doorway. He motioned her inside and then stood there for a bit, looking around.

"Anything wrong?" she asked, puzzled.

"I hope not," he answered. "Just making sure. There have been a few strange things and I've stepped up the video surveillance," he said, pointing to a tree across the drive. "I've got my eye on things, don't worry, darlin'," he said as he came inside.

Justin crossed the space between them and took Lauren into his arms. She clung to him; desperate for the strength she could draw from him. He kissed her and reluctantly released her because he knew she had come for a reason. "What's wrong?" he asked.

Sighing, Lauren flung herself down on the sofa and curled her legs beneath herself in a gesture of self-protection. Concerned, Justin sat down beside her and wrapped his arms around her. "Tell me," he urged.

"Anderson called me into his office when I came in this morning," she began.

299

"Oh?" Justin stiffened, waiting for her to go on.

"He told me there's to be an investigation by the AG's office into Bartley's death," she continued.

"Go on," Justin urged.

"He told me point blank that I was to avoid having an opinion or knowing anything at all about it. He made it clear in no uncertain terms. In fact, I think you could consider it a threat," she added.

Justin stood up, went to the panorama windows and kept his back to her. "What did you tell him?" he asked quietly after a few moments.

Lauren shrugged. "I said the only thing I could, that I didn't know anything and that I understood what he wanted."

"Is that all?" Justin asked.

"Almost. I took Betsy aside and told her to find me anything and everything she could on Bartley, but to keep it off the office computers." Lauren noticed Justin's stance now. "Why? What do you know?"

Justin said nothing. "You know something, Justin. Tell me what you know." Lauren jumped up and grabbed him by the arm, turning him around to face her. "Tell me what you know," she repeated.

"Lauren, at this point, the safest thing for you is to *not* know anything at all. You're going to have to trust me on this. I have connections, and I might know things, but for right now, you are being kept in the dark. If you are questioned by the AG's office, not only must you maintain plausible deniability, but Anderson will try and trip you up. He's bad news, Lauren, believe me. I'm protecting you."

Lauren's mouth was open to protest, but she knew he was right. Every instinct screamed that something was rotten in Denmark and Anderson was covering. It probably *would* be better if she didn't know what that was.

She nodded in agreement and Justin wrapped his arms around her, putting his chin on the top of her head. "Believe me, darlin'," he whispered. "Believe me when I say I would protect you with my life."

"Well, let's hope it doesn't come to that!" she protested but he pressed his finger against her lips.

"Of course," he said. "But you let me worry about this for now, promise?"

She hesitated a few minutes, unused to giving up her control. "Okay, I agree."

"Good, now give me a kiss and then I'm shooting you out of here. You're too enticing and I have things to do now that you've told me this."

She turned her face upward and met his lips. They were hard upon hers and she melted against him. "Enough," he said, easing her away and slapping her ass. "Take that beautiful ass of yours out of here before I lose control," he laughed.

"You'll be sorry," she said over her shoulder as she headed for the door.

"I already am," he answered.

CHAPTER THIRTY-SEVEN

Monica called Lauren's number and waited for the voicemail. She was surprised when Lauren picked up.

"Hi, Mon, what's up?" Lauren's voice was guarded and Monica was instantly on the alert.

"You sound funny," Monica said.

"Really? No, everything is fine."

Monica grunted delicately, "Sure, you are. I know when you're bullshitting me."

Lauren hesitated a long moment, knowing Monica was not to be put off. "Can't talk about it now."

Monica answered, "Yeah, that's just what I thought. Okay, it's about girl time so I'm calling Nikki. Where do you want to meet?"

Lauren sighed. The stress was getting to her and she wasn't sleeping well. She wasn't up to one of Nikki's drunken scenes and just wanted peace. "Tell you what, come by the house tonight about seven. Aaron won't be home and we'll curl up with a bottle of wine and just talk."

"Sounds good. I'll call Nikki and we'll see you then."

Lauren laid down her phone and sat back to think about what she would say to the girls. The secrets were starting to choke her. She didn't know who she could trust and who was out to get her. In some ways she wanted to throw it all away and just walk across a desert somewhere; somewhere that she could see anyone coming at her for a hundred miles around.

She busied herself for the next few hours with cases and it wasn't until just before she was leaving for the day that Betsy showed up in her doorway. "May I come in?"

"Sure, come in and shut the door," Lauren said, noting that Betsy held a thick manila envelope.

"I have this for you, Lauren," Betsy held out the envelope. "I kept it in my case until I saw you were about to leave. There's nothing here that anyone in this office has seen, no calls were made on these phones and there was no use of the office copier."

"I appreciate that more than you know," Lauren said, taking the bulky envelope. "Was there anything here that struck you as particularly odd?"

"Lauren, I'm not sure what I was supposed to be looking for so I really can't say. But if it exists in the open, it's in that envelope. Let me know if there's anything else I can do," she added, heading for the door.

"Betsy, thank you," Lauren said, tempted to open the envelope but knowing there was no way she could risk it here in the office, so she slipped it into her tote and finished getting ready to leave. She picked up her phone and ordered a gift basket for Betsy including a day at the spa, chocolates, flowers and a variety of perfumes, lotions and makeup.

Lauren opened the door to find Monica and Nikki standing there. Nikki was clutching three two-liters of soft drinks and Monica held out a bottle of rosé. Lauren looked puzzled and Monica smirked, "She's on the wagon," and stepped into the foyer. Nikki followed dutifully and was wearing jeans and a fisherman's sweater that was many sizes too large for her thin form.

"Nikki," acknowledged Lauren. "You're looking...different," she added.

Nikki smiled sweetly and proceeded through to the kitchen where she got a tall glass from the cupboard, filled it at the ice dispenser and poured a full share of cola.

Lauren looked at Monica for explanation, but she merely shrugged and poured two glasses of wine; one of which she held out to Lauren. "Well, c'mon in and let's sit in the solarium," Lauren invited, leading to the sunny room at the back of the house that opened out to the patio. It was filled with flowers and tropical plants, dotted with miniature fountains and wind chimes. A small koi pond sat at one end. This was Lauren's favorite room in the entire house.

"So, Nikki, what gives with the Mother Teresa getup?" Monica got right to the point.

"I'm starting over," Nikki said clearly, sitting stiffly upright when she more commonly slouched in among pillows. "I'm tired of my reputation and out to make something better of myself."

Monica rolled her eyes. "Who is he?" she asked immediately and settled back to hear the latest story.

"You don't know him," Nikki responded, but her eyes began to sparkle. "He's unlike anyone I've ever been with before. His name is Bradley, but naturally I call him Brad."

Lauren couldn't help herself. "Is he single?"

Nikki's eyes flared, "Of course! He's decent, better than I deserved and I will become a woman who is worthy of him."

Lauren hid her smile and sipped her wine at the same time. She was used to Nikki's fad moods and assumed this one would wear off in time as well.

Monica knew Nikki's moods as well and was more interested in talking about what was going on with Lauren. "So, spill it," she said, putting the glass of wine on the table. "What the hell has gotten into you lately?"

Lauren drew a deep breath. "Just hear me out on this, okay?"

The girls nodded. Monica knew already she wasn't going to like what she was about to hear, but it may as well get said.

Lauren began. "Things have not been going well at work. One of our clients, my client to be precise, killed himself and Anderson is acting strangely. He has made it no secret that he doesn't want me around, but I have the rest of the board's support, so for the time being, they want to keep a pretty face on things." She drew a breath.

Nikki urged her. "Go on…"

"Well, there's Aaron. He has been behaving strangely, disappearing at odd hours without explanation, acting tired all the time like he not resting at night."

"Well, is he?" Monica prodded.

"What?" Lauren asked.

"Is he sleeping?"

Lauren hesitated a moment and then answered, "I don't know. I've been in the guest room for some time now. He paced all night and was keeping me up."

Monica's eyes grew wide. She knew what separate rooms signaled.

Lauren continued. "I saw Aaron outside a large office building downtown. He had no reason to be there...no clients there, no one I know. He had to be seeing someone on the sly. He didn't see me and by the time I parked, he had disappeared. He has been up pacing all night, like something is really bothering him. We haven't talked about it, but I think he's seeing someone and wants to just have an open marriage.

The girls' eyes were huge. Aaron was the last person they imagined who would cheat. He was like the poster boy for integrity in their opinion.

"That it?" Monica interrogated.

Lauren shook her head and took a deep breath. "There's this guy…"

"Oh, shit, here it comes," Monica burst out. "I knew there was a dick in the mess somewhere."

Nikki's eyes were huge. "I don't understand. Lauren, girl of any of us, you're the one we depend on to stay the course. You're not supposed to be anything other than perfect!"

Lauren felt herself flushing with embarrassment. "Before you judge me, you should know that I've been followed, and probably still am. Justin…he's the guy…Justin is a paralegal in the office, but not just that. He's from a well-connected family and is well…let's just say he doesn't want anything to happen to me. He's been looking out for me. I trust him, and right now that can't be said of too many people." She paused for a break.

Monica burst first. "Lauren, I don't give a rat shit's ass who is following you. You have a husband and it's his job to take care of that department until such time as he tells you otherwise, whore or no whore! Aaron is a good man and I don't believe he's chasing skirt; I just don't believe it. So you better sure as hell clamp those legs together and keep it at home. Nikki here ain't got anyone…"

Nikki sat up and raised a finger to protest, but Monica was on a roll.

"…and my man has papers to show he's been walking out on me. You are spreading your legs just because you're ornery and want to; don't you blame it on work or Anderson or most of all Aaron! I've had enough of this shit! You sit there all high and mighty, Miss Lawyer of the Year crap, marries well, gets into a law firm right away, and this is what you do with it? I thought you had class, girl…but all you got is ass!"

With that Monica stood up, grabbed her bag and headed for the front door. Nikki, sheepish, but unwilling to take on Lauren by herself, followed.

The door slammed behind them and with them, the only sanity Lauren figured she still had in the world.

CHAPTER THIRTY-EIGHT

There was a short knock on Anderson's door before it opened and one of the partners and board members, Stanley Shore, slipped into the room.

Anderson looked up and his face melted into a quasi smile, or at least as close to one as anyone could tell given the enormous girth of his head. "What brings this unexpected pleasure?" he asked, motioning to Stanley to have a seat next to the desk. "I wasn't sure I would hear from you again."

Stanley behaved nervously, taking the seat and then leaping up immediately to go to the window and look out. He stood with his back to Anderson and said, "I wasn't sure I wanted to see you outside the boardroom again, to tell you the truth."

Anderson heaved to his feet and walked over to place his hands on Stanley's shoulders. "I'm sorry to hear that. I thought we could get past all that nastiness by now."

Stanley turned. "Is it over? Is it safe yet?"

"Almost, Stan," Anderson said softly and cupped Shore's face in his meaty hand. "Did you miss me?"

"You know I always missed you. You know I hated what you made me do." Stanley's eyes showed glints of tears and he tipped his head sideways so that his cheek lay in the palm of Anderson's hand. "Please don't ever make me do that again," he pleaded.

"I won't. It was the first, and the last time, Stan. It was just something that had to be done and now, it's all behind us and we can get on with the things we want most in life." Anderson's voice was soothing, as if talking to a child. "You do trust me, don't you?"

Stanley nodded, his eyes pleading with Anderson for understanding and reassurance. "You know how much I love you, right?" Anderson nodded. "And you know I'd die a thousand times for you if it meant you would be happy, right?" Anderson nodded again. "Then where do we go from here?"

Anderson pulled his hand back slowly and returned to the stability of his chair. His legs were often stiff

313

and sometimes numb from supporting his weight and he could seldom stand for more than a few moments before he began to sway and needed a support to lean against. "Stanley," he sighed. "I will let you know when the time is right. There are some investigations being conducted by the AG's office and we need to keep low until they're done sniffing around."

Shore frowned at this. "Are they going to talk to me?" he asked.

"That depends. Will they think they *need* to talk to you?" Anderson asked. "Did you leave a trail?"

"Oh, no, Mason, truly I didn't. I did everything exactly the way you told me. It all points to the bitch; none of it to you, and not to me. As far as anyone knows, we are just attorneys in the same office, nothing more. I swear," he ended, nervous in Anderson's suspicious gaze. Shore sat down in the chair once again and crossed his legs. He leaned forward toward Anderson, wanting to soak up a bit of reassurance for his efforts.

Anderson straightened momentarily and said, "Alright Stanley. You go for now and keep your mouth shut. It will all blow over soon and then you'll have everything I promised, okay?"

Shore nodded, seemingly reassured and arose from the chair. He turned before he left and whispered, "I love you, Mason."

Anderson looked up and tried to smile. "I know you do, Stanley, I know you do," he said in a gravely whisper. "Now run along like a good boy."

Shore nodded again and left, closing the door behind himself with the delicacy of a small child. Anderson frowned and shook his head. *The fools I have to suffer* he thought to himself.

He then picked up the phone and called the same number he had been forced to ring so often lately. "Anderson here," he said curtly into the speaker. "I want a tail put on Shore. No, doesn't need to be a top man. Shore is a fool and won't suspect, much less notice. Just put somebody behind him to make sure he keeps his mouth shut and does the normal shitty crap he does each and every pitiful day of his life." With that he disconnected and smiled to himself. *Dealing*

with fools could be simple, or your worst nightmare.
Thank god I know how to handle them.

CHAPTER THIRTY-NINE

Lauren was sitting in her office when Betsy walked in the door. "Here's the end of it, Lauren," she said, handing Lauren another manila envelope. "Same as last time."

Lauren looked up and took the envelope, noting the bulk. "Betsy…"

"I know, don't say anything. I wanted to be thorough. There was far more than what I expected. I hope now that it's what *you* expected." Betsey turned to go, "And thank you for the gifts. They were lovely," she said over her shoulder.

"Thank *you*, Betsy," Lauren answered and slipped the manila envelope into her tote. She smiled at Betsy through the glass just as a FedEx man showed up and Betsy signed for a package. She had a quizzical look on her face as she came into Lauren's office again.

"I don't know why this was delivered directly instead of going through the mailroom, but the man said I had to personally sign for it. It's addressed to you, in care of me." She held out the box. "Do you think it's safe?"

Lauren considered this for a moment and then nodded. "It will be fine, I promise. Just leave it on my desk."

Betsy nodded and did as she was told. She left promptly and Lauren slid the slender box into her tote as well. She popped into the tiny bathroom adjoining her office and reapplied her lipstick. Grabbing her purse and tote, she smiled at Betsy on her way out of the office.

Once in the parking garage, Lauren removed the package and taking it, got out of the car and walked to the opening of that level in the garage. She shook the box and it made no sound. She reached into her pocket for the tissues she had put there and using them to cover her hands, opened the box. As soon as she had, she relaxed and smiled. There was a note in Justin's hand lying on top.

This is clean and the only number on it dials mine, which is also clean. When this is over, throw it away, but always, always keep it with you until then.

Lauren realized Justin had gotten them throwaway cells phones so they could talk and not be tracked. She slid hers down into her bra and it made her feel loved and protected to feel its cold metal case against her breast.

She threw the packaging in the bin across the street and headed home, but changed her mind and headed to the library instead. There she found a quiet, empty side room with a long table. She sat and spread the papers from the manila envelopes apart to begin studying them.

She sorted the papers into piles; news clippings, legal documents, copies of deeds and other mortgage papers, copies of certificates, printouts from the Internet, credit checks, background checks, even a copy of Bartley's passport. Her eyebrows rose at Betsy's thoroughness and she made a mental note to send Betsy a much nicer thank you this time. Bartley, himself, would have been impressed with the picture of his life that was spread across that library table.

Lauren spent almost three hours combing through the papers; every so often touching her hand against the phone that lay against her breast beneath the fabric of her blouse. It reassured her.

Finally, her face lit and her eyes grew bright. It was all there. All the evidence she needed. She tapped her fingers on the incriminating documents, deciding what to do with them. She was tempted to make copies while at the library, but copies could fall into the wrong hands. Instead, she paper clipped the important papers she needed most and slid everything back into the original envelopes.

She left the library and headed straight for the bank where she kept her personal stash of cash. In her opinion, every woman should have a personal stash; she might never know when it could be necessary to make a move that her husband might not approve of. Inside, she secured a safety deposit box and put the manila envelopes into the metal case.

Her next stop was to the post office where she took out a postal box with only her name on its card. She bought a small, padded envelope, addressed it to herself at the new PO box, slid the deposit key inside and stuck it in the mail slot.

Feeling triumphant, Lauren headed home. Aaron was waiting for her when she opened the door.

"Monica was here," he said bluntly. "She said she came to see you but wanted to talk to me first," he told her. "I'd like you to sit down and we need to talk," Aaron said.

Lauren's heart began to hammer. She was fairly sure she could trust Monica, but a pissed Monica was something else entirely.

Lauren sat and kicked off her shoes, doing her best to appear nonchalant. "So, what's up?" she asked.

Aaron sat in the chair opposite hers and while he did not remove his shoes, he did lean back, wincing as he did so.

"It seems Monica had a few questions for me," he began.

"Oh? What would she want with you?" Lauren asked.

"Well, it sounds as if somewhere or sometime she got the idea that I might be stepping out on you." Lauren choked a bit and flushed but Aaron kept on going. "Do you have any idea where she might have gotten that impression?" he asked calmly.

Lauren's mind flailed, searching for a non-committal answer that he would buy. She had thought she was in good shape now, having found the evidence she had sought. "I really don't know," she began.

"Come now, Lauren, let's be up front about this. Monica doesn't have any connection to me except through you and I'm fairly sure the information she has came directly from your mouth," he offered, his voice tense.

"Monica and Morgan are divorcing. She's seeing ghosts in every corner. Ignore her." Lauren was reaching.

"I don't think so, Lauren," he returned. "I think Monica must be mightily sure of her facts to ignore her own situation right now and pay attention to our lives. Why is she doing that?" he pressed.

Lauren sat in the chair, her head spinning and her stomach nauseas. *Is this the time to bring it all out? Do I dare?* She asked herself these questions and knew she had no choice. If she put it off, she lost the advantage of surprise.

Lauren stood up and walked into the foyer, returning with Aaron's phone that always lay on the side table. She pressed some buttons and skimmed her finger down a list of phone numbers.

"What are you doing?" Aaron asked, perturbed. "Isn't there something called privacy between us?"

"You would think so," Lauren countered, "except that it's not always deserved. It comes with trust, Aaron. Trust as in between a husband and his wife."

"So, when did I compromise that trust?" he wanted to know, his voice rising with anger. He was shifting in his chair, wincing at the same time.

"What are these numbers?" Lauren demanded, holding the phone face toward him yet firmly in her hand.

"What numbers?" he countered.

"These!" she handed him the phone and he looked at the face of it, his face growing pinched as he skimmed the long list.

"Where did you get these, Lauren?" he demanded.

"There's an app for that," she said in a mocking voice. "I put an app on your phone weeks ago and not only has it been tracking every call and every GPS location you've been, it has copied all that information to an account in my name. I have it all, Aaron. So what do you have to say for yourself?"

Aaron said nothing. He quietly turned off the phone, stood and walking past her without looking, went up the stairs to his bedroom.

Lauren stood there fuming. *Not only did he have the nerve to interrogate me, he didn't even say a word to defend himself!*

She sat again and fumed for a long time before finally opening her blouse and removing the phone Justin had sent her. She dialed the only number in its contact list. "Meet me at the park," was all she said and then flipped the phone off and slid it back into her bra.

Justin pulled in just a few minutes after her. He pulled up next to her, got out of his car and slid into her front seat. She leaned to kiss him but he held back. "Not in public, darlin'," he cautioned and buckled the seatbelt. "There are people watching."

Instead he directed her to pull out into traffic and eventually they found themselves riding through the country where the roads were deserted and it was far more difficult to be followed without detection.

Lauren found a public access on a small lake and pulled into the parking lot. She reached to shut off the ignition and then into her purse to extract a key.

"This goes to a post office box and inside is an envelope addressed to me that contains a second key to a safety deposit box." She kept her voice solemn and tried not to show too much emotion. She felt drained. "This key will always be in this glove box," she pointed to the one at his knees. "The number is PO Box 3876 at the main branch. If something should happen to me, I want you to get this key, get the

325

envelope and read what is inside. It has everything you will need to incriminate the person responsible." She looked straight ahead out of the windshield and told him the name of the bank where the safety deposit box rested.

"Lauren! What have you been up to? You'll get caught and they won't blink before disposing of you! How could you be so reckless?" Justin was angry. She had taken unnecessary chances and he didn't like it one bit.

"Never mind that, Justin. With you out of the office, I'm the only one in a position to look after myself there and that's what I'm doing."

"Don't do another thing, do you understand me?" Justin was more than angry. He sat there several long minutes huffing before finally asking, "So, what sort of evidence and who does it incriminate?"

"It's just as you suspected," was all she would say. "I don't want to say any more than that. *Plausible deniability,* remember?" she repeated the phrase he had used with her before.

"Not good enough," he answered curtly.

"Doesn't matter, Justin. It's all you're going to get for now. I can handle it from here on out and in fact, I'm the only one who is in a position to do it. You'll just have to trust me."

"There is a lot at stake here, Lauren," he cautioned.

"Don't tell me!" Lauren was angry it burst from her before she could consider the consequences. "Don't tell me," she repeated in a softer voice and then burst into tears.

Justin wrapped his arms around her and let her cry against his chest. He stroked her hair and patted the back of her head. "Now, tell me what's going on," he urged once she had calmed down.

"It's Aaron," she said, her words making him stiffen. "I know he's been with at least one other woman and I've caught him at it."

"Really?" Justin was shocked. "How? What happened?"

Lauren sniffed and he pulled a tissue from her purse and handed it to her. "I've been tracking his cell phone from an app. I have all the evidence in a locked account with password protection. He's been gone at all hours, is tired all the time like he's up all night, and is going places he has no reason to be. I'm not a fool, Justin. I know what's going on."

"I see," was all he said, thinking to himself. "What do you plan to do about it?" he was almost afraid to ask.

"I don't know. First things first. I have to get myself out of this mess and straight with the AG's office before I deal with Aaron. So, for now, I'm keeping the information to myself. Only you and the girls know about it. Monica took it upon herself to come by and have a talk with him tonight and now he's aware that I know," she sniffed loudly.

Justin hesitated only moments before asking, "What did he say?"

"Oh he confronted me, trying to turn it on to me, as though I'm the one who should be guilty about something. He knew he had been caught and he went on the offensive to buy time. We're not talking."

"I see," Justin said again, thoughtful. He knew better than to get in between Aaron and Lauren. She would have to make her own decisions on this...and while he could hope for a certain outcome, it would be hers to bring about. He was too busy watching her back when it came to Anderson.

"When are you coming back to the office?" she asked, changing the subject.

"I'll be there Monday," he answered. Anderson left me a message to show up. The AG's office will be coming in and it could look suspicious, I suppose, if I weren't there, considering I worked with you on the case while Bartley was still alive.

Lauren nodded. It made sense. She felt like walls were closing in around her. She blew her nose and pushed back from Justin, starting the engine. She drove him back to the park and with a squeeze of his hand out of view, he slid out and left in his car while Lauren returned home. Aaron's light was dark and his

329

bedroom door shut. He never shut the door unless he was inside.

Lauren tiptoed past the closed door and entered her own room, showering quickly before she slid into bed and falling immediately asleep.

CHAPTER FORTY

Lauren settled herself in the solarium and tapped Monica's number. She needed to resolve their conflict now before things went any further.

"Hello?" Monica's voice was remote and cool.

"Mon?" Lauren began.

"Yeah, you called me." Monica wasn't going to give in easily.

"Okay, so I know you're pissed," Lauren went on.

"You could say that, bitch," Monica snarled.

"You don't know how it's been and Aaron's been screwing around for quite a while," Lauren justified.

"Says you," Monica responded. "He told me he hadn't seen anyone but you since you met. Ya wanna address that one?"

"Yes, I do, as a matter of fact. Where do you get off coming over here and telling him that? Do you have any clue what a boundary is? Who the hell is your friend, anyway...Aaron or me?"

"It's not about friends, Lauren. It's about doing the right thing. And you ain't."

"Monica, you're being hard on me because of Morgan," Lauren countered.

"Leave him outta this!" Monica shouted over the line. "You don't know what you're talkin' about and I didn't invite you to voice any opinions as far as I know," she added.

"Perhaps you should take your own advice, Monica," Lauren said stiffly. "Look. We girls tell each other things and it's not supposed to go any further. That's girls' code and you know it. You can't break that and expect to still get it in return."

"Don't tell me the rules, Lauren. I'm not the one breakin' them."

"Okay, I can tell we're not going to get anywhere with this. Can we just agree to disagree and move on?

Your friendship is more important than anything to me and I really don't want to fight with you," Lauren pleaded.

There was a long silence on Monica's end and Lauren thought perhaps she had hung up. "Mon?"

"I'm here." Monica's voice was odd and Lauren knew she was crying. Rather than aggravate her further, she said nothing and just waited for Monica to gather herself.

"Lauren, I don't want to fight either. It's hell here. Morgan's daddy is sick and he needs me...he's got nobody else to look after him. I'm like his daughter."

"I know you've always been good to him," Lauren interjected.

"How am I supposed to take care of him and divorce his son at the same time?"

Lauren waited a moment before asking, "Are you really sure you want a divorce? Is there no way you can get past this?"

Monica huffed. "You must've been talkin' to Morgan. He says the same thing. He keeps buggin' the shit out of me to go back to him."

"And?"

"And what? What kinda life is that? Who wants to be married to, and maybe have kids with someone they can't trust? You, maybe...but not me."

"That's not fair, Monica."

"Life ain't fair, sweetie. You been around long enough to know that one." Monica was being cynical; a sure sign that her feelings were mixed on the topic. "So?"

"So...so what?" Lauren responded.

"You gonna leave that Justin alone and stay with your man where you belong?" Monica was not going to give up.

"That's not fair. Aaron started this. I don't know what I'm going to do, but I'm not filing any papers any time soon, I know that much. I've got too much else going on—hell, my entire career is on the line right now."

Monica was quiet for a minute. "We both got our problems, don't we?" Her voice was ragged. "I can't sleep anymore. I think I know what I'm goin' to do and then I go see Morgan's daddy and I fall apart inside. I want a baby so bad. If I have to start all over to find a husband and daddy, it could be too late for me, forever."

"Don't say that, Monica. You're still young and there are all kinds of ways to have children. Go get your eggs frozen."

"I'm waitin' for Hell to freeze over before I do that!" Monica cursed. "I'm goin' to have a baby and it's goin' be the natural way, so help me God."

"I get it. How's Nikki?" Lauren asked after a pause.

"You know Nikki," Monica sighed.

"Well, actually, no I don't seem to any more. She's so different from what she's always been. Who is this new man she's hooked on?"

"His name is Brad-ley…" Monica mocked.

"So I hear, but where did she meet him? Who is he?" Lauren's curiosity was piqued.

"How do I know? She hardly says anything any more. She's all over the high road and acts like she's a nun. Whoever he is, I hope he can keep her out of trouble when this goodie two shoes act she's pullin' falls apart. She'll get bored, you mind my words."

"You're probably right," Lauren agreed. "But in the meantime, let's not push her back off the ledge. As long as she behaves herself, let's support her."

"Uh, huh…" Monica agreed.

Lauren thought for a few moments and burst out, "I know!"

"What?" Monica asked.

"I think it's about time I do a little entertaining. What if I have a dinner party—you know a nice buffet, catered affair… You can bring who you want, Nikki can bring Brad-ley…" she said, mimicking Monica's tone.

"And who you gonna bring?" Monica asked sarcastically.

"Don't be a bitch, Mon, it doesn't flatter you."

"So when is this affair you're planning goin' to be?"

"I'm thinking a couple of weeks. I can call a caterer tomorrow and set it up. We'll throw together some invitations and I'll have Betsy send them out tomorrow. I'll invite some people from the office just to keep Aaron entertained and Nikki can bring her new man."

Monica was silent.

Lauren asked the hard question, "Do you want to bring Morgan?"

Monica didn't answer for long moments. "I'll think about it," she said finally. "Can I invite Morgan's daddy?"

"Of course!" Lauren answered enthusiastically. "The more, the merrier."

"Good. Now get busy. I've got some dress shoppin' to do!"

"Mon?"

"Yeah?"

"I love you."

"Love you too, bitch," Monica responded and the line went dead.

CHAPTER FORTY-ONE

Lauren hurried through her dressing the next morning, excited at the prospect of having a dinner party. They hadn't entertained forever and she not only owed so many others a return invitation, but thought this would be an ideal time to heal many of the wounds and problems going on in her world.

She approached Aaron about it over a hurried breakfast of toast and juice. "It just sort of occurred to me at the spur of the moment. What do you think?" she asked him in an excited voice.

Aaron's face was sallow and she could tell he'd been up all night again. She decided to ignore it and that while she wanted him to approve of the party, she certainly didn't need his sanction.

"I think it's fine if it will make you happy, darling," he said in an accommodating voice.

She looked at him to gauge his sincerity and he seemed genuine. Her heart melted a bit and she wondered why he was straying. What was wrong with her that he needed to look elsewhere?

"I'll take care of the details," she said in an accommodating voice. "Betsy will do most of the inviting for me and I'll have it catered. I'll have someone in to clean and hire a bartender and serving staff for the night of the dinner."

"Sounds fine, darling," Aaron said, his back to her as he leaned on the kitchen counter.

Lauren frowned. "Are you alright?"

"Nothing," he said, if somewhat too quickly. "It's nothing, just a headache," he added.

Lauren upended her glass of orange juice and couldn't help saying, "Maybe you should get some more sleep."

Aaron said nothing so Lauren picked up her case and handbag and left for the office.

Lauren had Betsy and a cup of coffee in her office for a planning session. Betsy was extremely competent and enjoyed the break from her normal duties. Lauren knew she could rely on her.

"How about the guest list?" Betsy asked. "If this an office partners' affair?"

Lauren stopped to consider this. She had gotten so caught up in the excitement of the planning that she hadn't really taken time to consider the guest list.

"Well, naturally Aaron and I, Monica, Nikki and Nikki's new boyfriend, Brad. Monica and Morgan are having problems but invite Morgan and his father." Lauren mentioned a few other people who were clients of the firm, but friends at heart.

"How about people from the firm?" Betsy asked the hard question.

Lauren deliberated a few moments. She picked up a Post-it-Note™ and scribbled a few names on it. "Invite these partners, and these only." She handed the paper to Betsy.

341

Betsy looked it over. "Not Mr. Anderson?"

"No." Lauren's voice was succinct. "I might have to work with him, but I don't have to feed him at my table."

Betsy looked doubtful, as if Lauren were committing professional suicide. "It's okay," Lauren said. "I know what I'm doing." She looked up and saw the worried look on Betsy's face. "Just do it, Betsy." Betsy nodded and stood to go. "Oh, and Betsy?"

Betsy turned and Lauren said, "Add your name to that list." Betsy's eyes widened and she nodded slowly.

Lauren turned to her computer and began looking for party decorations. She wanted new glassware and table linens. This party had to really be something special.

Betsy tapped at the door and stepped inside when Lauren looked up. "Did you intend to invite Mr. Wilder?"

Lauren's heart dropped as she said the words, "Leave Justin off the list."

The night of the dinner party had arrived. Everything had been pulled together quickly and efficiently with the help of professionals and Lauren was quite satisfied with the results. The R.S.V.P.s had been returned with 100% acceptance.

Lauren was in her room, preparing to dress when Aaron tapped at her door. "How's it going, darling?" he asked congenially.

Lauren was busy deciding which gown to wear and going over all the last minute details in her mind. Her response was absent-minded. "Fine, fine. Go and get dressed now. Our guests will begin arriving in an hour. I'll need you downstairs to greet them if I'm tied up with something," she added.

Aaron nodded, took a look at her long, lovely back and closed the door softly before heading off to his own shower.

Lauren had chosen a gown of raspberry silk, trimmed in a handmade black lace that barely covered her thighs. She applied matching nail polish and swept her hair upward into a simple twist before fastening a diamond clasp to hold it in place. Black, stiletto heels completed her outfit and she looked in the mirror and was satisfied. Her long, graceful neck was encircled with a single strand of diamonds Aaron had given her for a birthday when they were first married. It had been a huge expense for him and they promised one another it was a symbol of their future success. It nestled in her cleavage and the sparkle made her skin enticing.

By the time she made it downstairs and checked in with the catering staff, the doorbell began to ring. Aaron answered it and she could hear his voice as he welcomed guests inside. She made her way to the foyer and found Nikki and Brad there. Nikki made the necessary introductions and Lauren was amazed. She liked the way Brad looked and handled himself. Oddly, Nikki seemed to have come up with a winner for once in her life. Lauren hoped they would make it.

Immediately after Nikki arrived, Monica was at the door and Morgan and his father trailed behind her. Lauren could tell Monica had been crying, but decided not to call attention to it. Monica was going through enough and if she chose to talk about it, she would.

One by one the guests arrived and the atmosphere was lively with spirited conversation and clinking glasses. They were almost to the point where dinner was to be served when the doorbell rang one more time.

Puzzled, Lauren went to answer it. She had done the count and everyone had already arrived.

She opened the heavy door to reveal the corpulent face and form of Mason Anderson.

"Hello, Lauren," he said in a mock cheerful voice. "My invitation seems to have gotten lost in the mail so I hope you don't mind my just coming without it?"

"Hello, Mr. Anderson," Lauren choked out. "Of course, come in. May I take your coat?" she asked, holding out her hand.

As Anderson cleared the doorway and turned to slide his coat off, another figure stepped forward from the shadows into the candlelit foyer.

"Hello, Lauren," he said.

Lauren smiled and looked up in surprise. She blanched when she recognized his voice and the sight of him confirmed it.

"I've brought a date, I hope you don't mind," Anderson swaggered in.

"Of course not," Lauren stuttered and held her hand out to Justin. "It's nice to see you; it's been a long time," she said in a purposefully loud voice.

"I hope you don't mind my barging in," Justin responded, looking over her shoulder to where Aaron stood, a studied but controlled anger in his face and his stance. Justin hurriedly added, "I really had no choice. Mr. Anderson insisted," he finished.

Lauren's eyes nodded while she held her head perfectly still. "Please come in and make yourself at home," she said and passed beside him to close the door.

Aaron finally spoke up. "Anderson.... Wilder...good to see you both," he said in a voice that was mechanically polite. Suddenly the joy had gone out of the evening.

Lauren knew her life was about to change.

CHAPTER FORTY-TWO

The end will come on slippered feet...
their soles burned in Hell.

Lauren took this opportunity to disappear into the kitchen and ask the temporary staff to quickly convert the sit-down dinner into a buffet. They weren't prepared for the additional guests. Lauren's carefully executed seating plan had now been nullified, as well. There was almost no one she wanted seated next to Mason Anderson, and two people she did not want seated next to Justin; Aaron...or herself.

To make matters worse, there were at least three people in the group who were absolutely furious with her right now, and one who was gleefully gloating. Monica and Nikki picked up on Justin immediately and Lauren was studiously avoiding their glares as she flitted about in the role of hostess.

Aaron was tense and angry. Worse yet, he most definitely believed that he had been set up and that this

348

whole party was an excuse to get Justin inside their home and into their lives in some sort of palatable manner. She knew Aaron would think that if Justin were welcomed once as a guest, he would become a frequent visitor, even when Aaron wasn't at home, and that would lead to the expected occurrence of events.

Mason Anderson, on the other hand, was positively cocky in his lumbering sort of way. He knew he had put her in a position of jeopardy and he felt the role of triumphant superiority empowering his mind with all sorts of additional plans. Anderson felt all the more clever for having arranged this turn of events in front of some of their most important clients. He was insidious and someone she could not let out of her sight at any point in her future. She knew that.

Worse yet, Aaron did not know that. He saw this as Lauren's doing.

Justin, on the other hand, did know what Anderson was up to. She assumed he was there as a sort of beneficent protector; on one hand making Anderson happy, while keeping an eye on her welfare. Did he really think he could do something to protect her?

Lauren felt intense anger...with herself. How could she have not seen this coming? Her best friends, her lovers and her worst enemies were now all in the same room. *What the hell was I thinking?* While, naturally, she had not invited the enemies, she had set the stage, laid the dry straw and Anderson only had to bring the match.

The staff worked quickly to re-distribute the place settings and serving dishes into the semblance of a buffet. Appetizers were circulated through the rooms. It was a warm evening and the doors to the patio from the solarium had been thrown open to the night's air. The fountains spewed colored water into their copper basins; there were several plants conveniently blossoming in the solarium and tiny LED lights laced the shrubbery around the patio. It was a fairyland in appearance and under normal circumstances, people would have relaxed, had a bit much to drink, dined on excellent cuisine and the party would have been a success. Anderson came into the scene like a putrefied rat, casting filth and treachery everywhere he looked.

The guests were beginning to fill their plates and circulate throughout the house, alighting on chairs or in sofa groups to eat and chatter with one another. Nikki and Brad had found a pair of rattan chairs in the solarium and were deeply involved in their own personal conversation. Nikki looked especially lovely in a sea green, strapless dress that blended perfectly with the tropical motif of the cushion upon which she sat. Her normally defiant face was soft and shining with the aura of redeemed decency.

There was a pronounced tension in the rooms as people sought to find someone familiar with whom they could talk, while avoiding those they preferred to not acknowledge. Anderson beamed with satisfaction at having controlled Lauren's gathering, at her expense. At one point his cell rang and he stepped outside momentarily to take the call.

Lauren was straightening up the dishes at the table when Anderson walked in and announced in an overly loud voice, "Lauren, my dear, I'm sure you won't mind, but that call was most important. A colleague has arrived in town and since I'm here, I've invited him to join us." His face held a smirk of satisfaction and Lauren's face burned with additional resentment.

"Of course, he's welcome." *What else could she say?* Even Aaron seemed irritated at this latest addition. He felt completely at the whim of Lauren, Anderson and almost everyone else at his own dinner party. It was not to be borne.

"Lauren, could we have a moment?" Aaron said to her. Lauren nodded and followed him upstairs to his bedroom. Once inside, Aaron shut the door and motioned her to sit on the bed.

Morgan brought his father a plate and stood next to him as he ate. Monica had sat on his other side, keeping him company while Morgan filled the plate.

"Now, Monica, honey, you don't need to sit here and babysit an old man," Mr. Hammond said kindly, his deep brown eyes moist with the unexpected attention.

"Hush," she whispered. "You're the best looking guy in the room!"

"And you are, by far, the most beautiful woman," he returned the compliment with a gushing smile.

"I'll say she is," chimed in Morgan as he returned with the plate. "My wife is not only the most beautiful woman in this house, but in my life."

Monica looked up at Morgan to gauge his sincerity and saw that his eyes were full of love and pride. *Could I be so wrong?* she thought to herself. *Am I throwing away whatever version of happiness I've worked so long to have?*

"What's up with you two, anyway?" asked Mr. Morgan, sampling the salmon on his plate gingerly with a fork.

"Just a little spat, Daddy," Morgan answered before she could say anything more. "My girl's coming home again tonight, aren't you, Mon?"

Monica smiled for Mr. Morgan's benefit, but she said nothing.

"Aren't you, Mon?" Morgan repeated.

"Excuse me while I find the powder room," Monica said finally, setting her plate down on the table next to her chair and leaving the men behind.

"Will this take long, Aaron? We have guests, after all." Lauren was a bit impatient.

"I'm quite aware of that, and that's exactly why I want you here to talk. What was the idea of Anderson and Wilder? I thought you weren't inviting them? Is this part of some cock-eyed master plan you're implementing?"

Lauren was shocked. "Are you fucking crazy? Why on earth would I invite Anderson? He hates me and is trying to undermine me at every turn. He invited himself and he brought Justin with him. I had nothing to do with this!" She was angry that Aaron would give her such little credit.

"What is Wilder to you? Tell me the truth, Lauren." Aaron's voice was like steel and she knew

354

there was no way she could escape its knife-like edge. Aaron was too smart for that.

What can I say? she thought to herself. "Aaron, I don't think this is the time to talk about this," she began.

"When will it be?" he shot back. "There's never a good time to talk about it, Lauren. In fact, there are very *few* good times of any nature between us recently." Aaron's voice faltered with emotion and Lauren's heart ached with indecision.

"Aaron, you haven't been entirely up front with me, either," she began. "All those calls, those appointments with people that aren't business related. Would you like to explain those?" she countered.

"There's nothing to explain, Lauren. There's no one else in my life but you. There never has been."

"Oh, right...I'm supposed to believe that?" Lauren began to stand up but Aaron pushed her gently back onto the bed.

"Lauren, have I ever lied to you?" he demanded.

Lauren was angry with him for preventing her leaving and she lashed back. "Every one of those calls is a lie, Aaron. Of course you have!" At the same time, she knew she had never actually caught him lying to her; about anything.

"Those calls are not to women," Aaron said in a steady, deadly voice. Lauren glared up at him and at the same time, tears welled in her eyes.

"But the phone app recorded it..." she began faintly.

Aaron stood before her, his hands clenched into fists. The veins stood out on the sides of his neck and he was trembling. He took a step forward then and leaned down toward Lauren. With one hand he reached forward to touch the glittering diamond that lay nestled between her breasts. He touched it, his hand lifting it to test the weight and at the same time, his fingers slid downward, behind the folds of fabric and onto her breast. He caressed her skin, his index finger tweaking her nipple until it rose, hard and begging to be suckled. Despite herself, Lauren leaned forward just an inch that she might coax his hand to linger a bit longer. This was the Aaron she had missed for so long; the man who had captured her heart years before. He was a man of purpose, of experience...a man who could incite her to orgasm with simply a breath into her ear.

The hand lingered, for only a moment before leaving to move to the neckline of the dress. With one movement, he ripped the neckline open, exposing her breasts and the magnificence of her skin.

Lauren gasped; not at the rending of the raspberry silk, but at the vehemence of his action. Aaron had not displayed such emotion since he'd first met her and they had made love upon his classroom desk. This excited her immensely; this was the man she had idolized.

Aaron pushed her backward now and completed his mission, ripping the dress entirely down the front until she lay bare, only her black stilettos to accent her nakedness. He fell forward upon her, grasping her hips in his hands and forcing her legs wide and up over his shoulders. His mouth lowered and licked her cunt, slowly and with a sucking motion that Lauren thought would drive her mad. His fingers opened her labia as though laying open the petals of a virginal rose. The sensation was one of tenderness and ownership...sending chills down her spine in its possessiveness.

Lauren's head rolled from side to side; so intense was the reaction to his probing mouth. She could feel herself flood and Aaron lapped up her juices with a low groan of satiation. She looked downward to see his head buried in her pussy and thought she would faint from the image. He glanced up, his lips glistening from her juice and she extended both hands to pull him upward.

Lauren closed her eyes and the next sensation was that of Aaron's hot torso against her. His clothing was gone and there was only the muscled chest pressing hard against her blossomed nipples and his juice-sated lips coming down upon her mouth. She could taste herself on him and the effect was enormously seductive. She sucked at his lips, licked his eyelids and as he penetrated her mouth with his tongue, he entered her with his swollen penis. Aaron pushed hard and found his way home, to the back of her woman's tunnel.

Lauren gasped, despite herself; the long-forgotten sensation of Aaron filling her depth now magnified itself in layered memories of all the times they had been together in just this way. Her muscles clenched with volition of their own, holding him captive within her...stroking him with their serpentine motion until Aaron finally withdrew only long enough to breach her again. This time she was blossomed and pliant, welcoming the intrusion. She clutched him deeply, so much so that he needed no further sensation but erupted within her. She could not help but whimper a soft regret that it was so soon over, but took his hot fluids willingly, like a clay carafe soaking up musky ale.

They lay thusly as minutes passed and the voices of the guests below began to penetrate Lauren's reality. Mindful and startled, she pushed at Aaron to roll off that she might return to her guests. He did roll to the side, but scooped her against his chest in a smothering grip. His hand drew her head toward his mouth and he whispered furiously into her ear.

"Listen to me, and do not say a word. I will only say this one time so you'll not want to miss a single syllable. Do you understand?"

Lauren's head was trapped against his mouth and she could do little but nod in agreement.

"The calls, the appointments in strange places…all the things you damn me for were not to be with other women, Lauren. I never left you and thought I never would. Whatever you have with Wilder ends as of this moment, do you understand?" Lauren barely nodded; fear tightening her throat.

"I'm dying, Lauren. I have maybe six months, perhaps a little more." She stiffened and fought to break lose that she might look at him, but his vise did not relent. "Stay with me, Lauren. Give me a child to leave behind. I want what's owed me." Lauren struggled, frantic now, but he would not let go. "When I'm gone, Lauren…you can go to him."

Aaron shoved her away then, and as she cried out in protest, at the words she had heard and the loss of his touch at such a devastating moment, Aaron rolled from the bed and slid into his bathroom, the lock clicking her out.

She began to shake then, the enormity of what had just taken place fighting to become her reality. Shock set in, though, and she realized she must move. There was a discreet knock at the door and Betsy's voice could be heard softly saying, "Lauren...another guest has arrived and you *must* come down. It's important."

"I'll..." Lauren whimpered and cleared her throat for enough volume to be heard. "I'll be right down." Steps retreated down the hallway and Lauren gasped when she realized her beautiful cocktail dress laid upon the carpet in a grotesque mockery of its former self. Shaking, she opened Aaron's closet and wrapped herself in his robe, stealing down the hallway to her own room; her sanctuary that no longer held solace in this Hell.

She found a simple black caftan and sat at her vanity long enough to sponge at her ruined makeup. The diamond clasp that had so elegantly captured her hair now hung haphazardly amongst tangled strands. Lauren gently removed it and brushed her hair until it hung straight and flowed over her shoulders. She surveyed her image in the mirror; the blackened depths of Hell had found her at last.

With resolve, she stood and slipped on ballet slippers before leaving her room. Aaron's door was still closed, so she passed by and began to descend the stairway. Those who were standing nearby looked up to watch her, questions in their eyes.

"I'm so sorry," she fabricated. "I felt unwell and will need to retire and leave you all to your own merriments," she prevaricated.

Anderson stepped forward from the clustered guests, a triumphant smirk dimpling the corpulent chins above his wine-stained shirt. "Not so fast, my dear Lauren," his raspy voice sang out. "There's someone here to see you."

He stood to one side as a man in a rack-quality black suit stepped forward. "Mrs. Lauren Reynolds?" he inquired.

"Yes?" she responded automatically, puzzled.

"My name is Porting. I am representing the state attorney general's office in an investigation of the alleged suicide of a Mr. Alvin Bartley?"

Lauren was puzzled; the name of her late client flagging an alert deep within her shocked awareness. "Yes?" she invited him to continue.

"You are hereby notified that you have become a person of interest in our investigation and as such, you will be read your rights. If you will accompany me, please?" he indicated the door with his arm.

"What?" Lauren's expression was mixed bewilderment and angst. "I am...that is *was*...his attorney. There is nothing I can discuss with you and you know that."

"Ma'am, this falls outside client-attorney privilege and you are, shall we say, hereby under temporary arrest and to remain in my custody until you have been questioned. If you will..." he said again indicating the door.

Lauren felt her knees buckle and she desperately looked out over the guests for the one familiar face she could still depend on. Justin stood next to a potted palm, a glass of wine seeping onto the carpet at his feet. His face was full of pain and desperation; his eyes moist at the realization that there was nothing he could do to help her. At the same time, he had noted the familiar disheveled appearance he had so often brought upon her. He knew where she had been and with whom. Betrayal caused the muscle in his cheek to

363

lightly jerk...his nostrils flared in anger and disappointment.

"But...I don't understand..." Lauren stammered.

Anderson came toward her, his grotesquely obese gait guarded on the slippery tile of the foyer. He held out his arm and the smile on his face belied the generosity of the gesture. "Come, Mrs. Anderson...Lauren...your time has come."

CHAPTER FORTY-THREE

Lauren sat in the back seat of Anderson's Bentley and although she was not truly in captive custody, it didn't matter. She had nothing left to lose at this point; or at least she thought.

She was somewhat surprised when they pulled up to the law office instead of a police headquarters. But then, of course, a local officer hadn't arrested her. She must have looked puzzled because Porting turned in his passenger seat and said, "Mrs. Reynolds, while you are in custody at the moment, it is an unofficial action and I simply want to ascertain some facts from you. Should you cooperate, there is, I believe, no reason that this become official business."

The bastard! thought Lauren. *Anderson is behind this. He set up this show at my dinner party to humiliate me in front of my friends and clients, knowing fully well that he had neither warrant nor evidence to arrest me! It's his crony from the AG office who is here to do his dirty work! Justin warned me not to turn my back on Anderson and I thought I had it all under control. How could I be so wrong? Again?*

She was fighting hard not to think about Aaron and the emotions of those passionate minutes combined with the devastating confession. *Die? Aaron? It can't be true. There's something that can be done, surely. We've got money. We'll go to Switzerland or Australia or the Caribbean. Whatever it is, I know we can heal him.*

Her thoughts were interrupted as they pulled into the parking garage and the two men escorted her into the elevator and up to the firm's office.

"I'll be acting as counsel for you, Lauren," Anderson informed her.

"I prefer to act as my own," Lauren responded. The last thing she needed was for the serpent to guard her from his own nest of vipers!

"I don't think that would be in your best interest, Mrs. Reynolds," interjected Porting. "While I'm sure your prowess as an attorney is to be admired, it might

366

be better if you had someone else to act as your...shall we say...reference and benefactor?"

"What on earth are you talking about?" demanded Lauren. "What the hell are you cooking up to frame me with?" She was angry and she knew better than to say more. Anderson was making note of each comment she made, gauging how to use them as buttons for pushing down the line.

"If you please?" Porting had opened the door to the conference room and was indicating she should enter.

Lauren deliberated a few seconds and then walked in and took a seat at the head of the table opposite Anderson's chairman's seat. The shock of what she had been through over the past hour was beginning to wear off and tears were streaming down her face. She reached into her handbag and rummaged for tissues.

Porting took a seat near Lauren and opened his briefcase, removing a small, digital tape recorder and placing it with a firm hand on the space between them. He tapped a button and spoke, acknowledging the date, the name of the people in the room, the reason for the meeting and then asked, "Mrs. Reynolds, this conversation is being recorded and anything you say may be used in a court of law. Have you been read your rights or are you, as an attorney, waiving that reading?"

"Yes, I agree and yes, I know my rights," Lauren responded, defiant in her innocence. She knew, however, that innocence was not a guaranteed defense. The grandfather clock in the corner of the room sounded then, ten chimes to indicate the hour and to Lauren it sounded like a death knell. *Why have I never noticed that monstrous thing until now?* she asked herself. Suddenly the room felt close and hot. "May we open a window?" she requested.

Porting looked to Anderson for approval, who shrugged and said, "Why not? Let her have whatever remaining breaths of free air she can...they'll be gone soon enough." Lauren stood and went to crank open the window closest her seat. While there, she looked down below to the ground floor and watched as the headlights of passing cars exited the city. She knew these were probably couples, leaving their dinners at charming restaurants and heading for home and a few hours in one another's arms. They were so oblivious, so secure in their expectation that they would be protected while they slept naked and intertwined by the very people preparing to snuff out her freedom in this room. She drew in deep breaths of the air, as if storing it up for some future date when she might sample it again from within.

"Mrs. Reynolds, may we proceed?" Porting was becoming impatient. After all, it had been a long day and he was looking forward to the Florida vacation Anderson had promised him. He could already feel that new nine iron in his hand and had been at the driving range for weeks.

"Of course," Lauren replied and resolutely took her seat and placed her hands on the table. She made a rather incongruous picture in her black caftan and ballet slippers, covered by a belted trench coat.

"Would you care to give me your coat?" Anderson poked at her, but Lauren ignored him.

"Now, Mrs. Reynolds," Porting began, "you understand that there are some irregularities involved in the death of Mr. Alvin Bartley?"

"I have no idea," Lauren responded.

"Mrs. Reynolds, I can assure you it would be in your favor to accommodate this investigation and surely, if you have nothing to hide, there's no reason for you not to do precisely that." Porting sighed a bit, getting ready to do battle. Anderson had warned him she wouldn't be an easy target; she knew her stuff.

"I'm fully prepared to cooperate in whatever legal manner open to me, Mr. Porting. However, you should recognize that I am not familiar with any of the details regarding the death of Mr. Bartley." Lauren was resolute in her determination to tread carefully, no matter how emotional the turmoil going on inside her at the moment. She was, after all, a professional and above all things, had an innate inability to prioritize.

Porting tried another track. "Was Mr. Alvin Bartley your client?"

Lauren answered, "Mr. Bartley was a client of this law firm, of which I am a partner."

Porting tried again, "Were you primary counsel assigned to his case?"

"I was one of three individuals in this firm who had been asked to help Mr. Bartley, but it was under the direct and active supervision of Mr. Anderson, the firm's principal partner, as well as the remaining partners. The firm represented many of Mr. Bartley's dealings, most of which I had no personal familiarity."

Anderson was getting agitated. "Lauren, you know you were hands on with the Bartley case and quit trying to squirm out of it. You're involved in his death and you know it!" He stopped then, realizing what he had just said. "Stop the recorder, Porting. Stop it, I say!" With that, Anderson leapt with as much ability as his walrus-like physique would permit, from his chair and grabbed the recording device, throwing it to the floor and stomping on it.

"Mr. Anderson, I hardly think..." Porting began.

"Shut up! You're not paid to think! You're paid to do what I tell you to do, dammit!"

"Mr. Anderson..." Porting started to interrupt once again.

"Fuck you, Porting, you worthless piece of shit!" Anderson was livid, heaving with exertion.

Porting sat back now, daunted by the ferocity of Anderson's temper. There was still that Florida trip to consider, although now it might come with more of a blackmail aroma.

Lauren clutched the trench coat about her more closely; she had begun to shake with the exhaustion of the last few hours. Just then, the door to the conference room opened and in walked her husband...and right behind him was Justin.

Lauren's mouth dropped open and Aaron came to her, enveloping her in his arms and asking if she was okay. She nodded and Aaron glared at Anderson without saying a word. He then took a seat next to Lauren.

Anderson was livid. "Who asked you here, Reynolds? Get out! This doesn't involve you."

Lauren looked at Aaron and then back at Anderson saying, "I am hereby relinquishing my right to my own defense in favor of my new counsel, Mr. Aaron Reynolds."

Porting was about to open his mouth when Aaron held up his hand and said, "I have with me a witness whose testimony is critical to this discussion and I am hereby including him. Mr. Justin Wilder, will you please take a seat and tell the gentleman from the A.G.'s office what you know?"

Justin hesitated only a moment before nodding and taking a seat opposite Porting. He took a deep breath and began to speak.

"I believe the matter in question is the demise of Mr. Alvin Bartley and I'm here to explain my knowledge and connection with that event. I do so of my own free will and wave the reading of rights or independent counsel."

"You can't do that," Anderson sputtered, nearly in apoplexy. "Get out of here!"

Porting was beginning to doubt whether Anderson would make good on the golf trip and thought it prudent to suddenly become as professional as possible, just in case.

"Very well, Mr. Wilder, please explain," he said.

Justin took a breath and began. "Approximately two weeks ago, and I can corroborate that exact date if requested to do so, I was called into this very boardroom by Mr. Mason Anderson, the gentleman you see here at the end of the table. Mr. Anderson, as senior partner, was my boss. He informed me that I was to work under the supervision of Mrs. Lauren Reynolds, also here in this room, in the defense by this firm on behalf of Mr. Alvin Bartley. The client had been accused of embezzlement, fraud and a few additional charges; all of which could have, had he been found guilty, led to a lengthy imprisonment. Mr. Bartley was a man in his early 70s and that would have had a serious impact on his remaining life, obviously."

"Stop this!" shouted Anderson, although Porting held up his hand to silence the sputtering behemoth.

Justin continued. "Mr. Anderson knew I had not yet taken the bar and could only act in the capacity of paralegal. Nonetheless, he indicated that my job was on the line, so naturally, I complied. I also had the distinct impression that Mr. Anderson was trying to circumvent some legal realities in his quest to somehow damage the reputation of Mrs. Reynolds here, and I felt it a matter of integrity that I attempt to remotely mitigate what he intended." Lauren looked at Justin, her heart in her eyes, but he continued to look straight at Porting.

"Shortly thereafter Mr. Anderson called me into his office and instructed me to access certain records regarding the Bartley case which were stored in the computer database here at the firm's office. He gave me a list of figures, addresses, dates and names that he wished altered."

Anderson screamed, "Enough!"

Porting looked at Anderson and pointed to the smashed recorder on the carpet and Anderson acknowledged the lack of recording and relaxed somewhat.

Justin went on. "Since what Mr. Anderson was instructing me to do was clearly in violation of not only legal ethics, but the law itself, I took the measure of copying the original data to an external server off these premises; data which I can still access and will be happy to do under court order." Lauren's eyes opened and again Justin refused to look at her.

"I complied with Mr. Anderson's instructions, as not to do so would simply have resulted in my dismissal and being replaced by someone who would do his bidding."

"And these alterations you made, Mr. Wilder. How did these affect Mr. Bartley's case or the representation by Mrs. Reynolds?"

"They were calculated to lead to a certain conviction of Mr. Bartley and if, for some reason, that did not happen, Mrs. Reynolds would most certainly have been indicted for obstruction of justice and that would have resulted in her loss of credibility and certain disbarment."

"And you have the data to prove this?" Porting went on.

Justin responded, "I do."

Anderson cackled from his chair, somewhat mollified by the fact that even though there was no evidence of this meeting, at least the people in the room, and in particular Lauren Reynolds, were aware of his power and shrewdness.

Porting looked at Lauren. "Do you wish to lodge charges against Mr. Anderson, Mr. Wilder or this firm, Mrs. Reynolds?"

Before Lauren could say anything, Aaron spoke up. "We wish to make that a possible option but are willing to come to an agreement to avoid such scandal for the firm."

"Huh!" Anderson burst out, spittle flying on to the table's surface.

"Our terms are these," Aaron continued. "We are requesting that Mr. Anderson resign immediately as a partner in this firm and no longer practice law in any capacity. He is to sign a full confession which will be kept private and locked away, not to be released unless he commits any act which is intended to damage Mrs. Reynolds or the members of this firm, including Mr. Wilder. Furthermore, we will request that Mr. Wilder be exonerated from his complicity as he was acting under orders from the head of this firm at that time and took measures to not only mitigate the damage to Mrs. Reynolds, but to ultimately act as witness against Mr. Anderson."

"Hah! Bullshit, Reynolds. You don't have a leg to stand on! Only the witnesses in this room, each of whom have something to lose if all this comes out and I destroyed the recording we made of Lauren's statement. Now here are *my* terms. You, that bitch of a wife and that young buck who cuckolded you are to leave immediately and your keys stay on this table. Your personal effects will be sent along to you. You will face disbarment proceedings should you ever breathe a word of this. I will see to it personally."

Aaron smiled; an odd thing for a man to do who stood to lose what future he had left to him. "Lauren, were you made aware that the testimony you offered was being recorded?"

"Yes," she said.

"Mr. Porting, were *you* aware of the recording being made?"

"Of course," he said.

"Anderson, how about you?"

"What kind of shit are you trying to pull, Reynolds? Of course I was, and I'm also the one who destroyed it!"

"Mr. Wilder, you were aware that a recording was being made?"

"Yes, I was," Justin responded.

"Fine, then let the record show, Mr. Porting, that Mr. Anderson has willfully and with full intent of doing harm to those in this room, committed any number of felonies including obstruction of justice; the rest of which may be determined by your office upon a more detailed investigation."

With that, Aaron reached into his breast pocket and calmly laid his cell phone on the table. Lauren reached into her bag and pulled out her own phone, laying it next to Aaron's. "Mrs. Reynolds, did you telephone me, your counsel, just as these proceedings were to begin?"

"I did," Lauren said solemnly. "I dialed your phone knowing you would listen and not hang up. I also knew that your phone contained an app which records and relays all conversations to an account I have obtained, thereby providing legal proof."

"I believe, Mr. Porting, that since all the parties involved here were aware of the recording, or at least "a" recording, this will serve as evidence in a court of law?"

Porting nodded, his face ashen.

"Mr. Anderson?" Aaron looked toward the head of the table. Mason Anderson, however, could not speak. His face was flushed and he was wildly pulling at his collar, trying to loosen his tie and get some breath. "Justin, call 911!" Aaron ordered and then leapt to help Anderson as the giant, engorged monster fell to the floor, unconscious.

CHAPTER FORTY-FOUR

The EMTs arrived quickly, but were unable to get Anderson out of the building immediately because he was too large for their gurney. They had to call for a bariatric gurney and in the meantime, the technicians worked on him as he lay on the floor. They were fairly certain he had suffered a stroke because he had lost the use of one side of his body and could not speak. He had soiled himself and the scene in the beautiful boardroom with the ticking grandfather clock was that from a horror movie.

Porting had pulled Lauren, Aaron and Justin to the side in Aaron's office and announced, "Unless someone in this room has an objection, I will consider this investigation closed. The coroner's report verifies Bartley's death was a suicide, although there is some question as to whether it was voluntary. The people in this room know without question who the only man capable of such manipulation might be, and the fact that he is incapable of even speaking, much less returning to a prosecutable condition, causes me to suggest that we drop this matter here and now. Mr. Wilder, if you will please make available a copy of the evidence you have in the event you leave our jurisdiction?" Justin nodded.

"Mrs. Reynolds, you have the A.G.'s office's sincere apology for what you have been through this evening. Needless to say, while I technically did nothing wrong, I will be the first to admit off the record that I came very close to doing so. It is coming up on my retirement and I doubt any of you will ever hear from me again. With that, I leave you," he said, snapping shut his case and disappearing among various medical equipment and personnel scattered about the office waiting room.

Aaron took one look at Lauren and knew she needed to go home. "Justin, as a gentleman, I'm going to ask you to take Lauren home before she collapses. Someone from the firm has to stay here until Anderson is moved. I will call a couple of the other partners, but for now, she needs rest."

Justin nodded and after Aaron hugged Lauren one last time, the two left the office and got into Justin's car in the parking garage. Neither said a word until Justin merged onto the expressway.

"Are you okay?" he asked, his hand on her leg.

Lauren nodded. "For now," she said but only she knew what she meant by that.

She closed her eyes for just a moment and suddenly the car's slowing and the bump of a rain curb awakened her to see they were pulling into her driveway.

Justin put the car in park and turned toward her. "Lauren, I just want you to know that nothing I did was intended to harm you."

"I know that," she said, nodding.

"You know now what Anderson was capable of doing. I couldn't refuse him and be banished beyond where I could help you. I had to do as he asked."

"I know, darling...I know. You had no choice. But Justin, you could have risked your entire career over that. Had it gotten out, you would have never been permitted to take the bar." She reached out and laid her hand on his cheek. He turned his face and kissed her hand and then pulled her against his chest. His arms held her tightly and his hand petted her hair. He spoke into her hair, kissing her forehead as he did so.

"Well, I *did* want to be a doctor," he joked awkwardly. "I just feel so guilty," he uttered. "Guilty and helpless."

"I know. You have nothing to be guilty for, Justin. I don't want to hear any more about it. Your life will be back to normal now and so will mine. Anderson is definitely out of the picture."

"No, Lauren. You're wrong." He held her tighter against his chest. "Aaron knows about us. I can tell."

She nodded her head against his chest. "Yes, he does."

"Don't you see?" his voice rose in optimism. "Darlin' we can finally be together! Aaron knows and this whole ordeal, if nothing else, gave us each something to hold over one another's head. He won't lift a finger to stop you from divorcing him. Then you will be mine! Sweetheart, this is what we've waited for!" He chuckled in joy and clutched her even more tightly.

"I love you so much, Lauren. I never thought you would be mind, truly mine!" his voice said deep from within his chest. He tipped her chin up and kissed her passionately on the mouth, his hand clutching the back of her head to keep her close to him.

"In fact, why not just go in and pack a few things and come home with me? What you don't pack, we'll buy. What we can't buy, you won't need anyway because I plan to keep you barefoot and pregnant for the next five years." Justin's joy and excitement was as delighted as a child with a new bicycle for Christmas. He could hardly believe how well it was working out; all the pressure from the firm; all the threats from Anderson were gone now. They were free to be together forever.

Lauren was shaking and puzzled, Justin looked down at her, wiping her hair away from her face so he could look into her eyes. "Darlin', what's the matter? Are you crying? Oh, my poor baby, you've been through so much. Forget the clothes, let me just take you home with me now and wrap you in my arms." He put a foot on the brake and a hand on the gearshift to slide the car into reverse.

Lauren's hand snaked out of the trench coat and gripped his arm, preventing him from shifting.

"What's wrong?" he asked, smiling in anticipation.

"I'm not going," she said, the tears streaming down her cheeks.

"Darlin', you'll feel much better in the morning. You're just in shock right now. I'll take care of you," he said, attempting the gearshift again, but she did not relinquish her grip.

"No! Justin, listen to me." Lauren was sobbing openly now, the coat and caftan falling open to reveal the curve of her breasts and the tender skin beneath them.

Justin looked at her like that; vulnerable, crying, so very feminine and so very, very alluring without even knowing it. He wanted to take her right there, in the car, right then.

Lauren put her hand up onto Justin's cheek. "Listen to me," she said softly. "This is going to hurt."

Justin frowned, not following what she was talking about.

Lauren sobbed a little more and then spoke. "Tonight, when Aaron and I went upstairs…"

"Stop there, Lauren. I could tell what happened. But that was before. I didn't want to think about it, but I always knew you were probably still making love with him. It's over. Done! You're mine now!"

"Listen!" she said, more forcefully than she wanted to. "Aaron is dying."

Justin looked at her, not absorbing what she was saying. His eyebrows were arched, "What do you mean, dying?"

"I mean literally, dying. Maybe six months, maybe a little more."

"What? Lauren, you're tired and you've been dreaming. Sweetheart, just lie back and close your eyes and I'll have us home in no time," Justin was frantically trying to rationalize her words.

"No, Justin. I know what I'm saying. He's sick. I don't know exactly what, but he hasn't long to live. I've known for a long time that something wasn't right, but thought he was just worn out from having affairs at night. All those times I thought I caught him sneaking off to someone's apartment...he was visiting doctors. Aaron is dying, Justin. It's that simple."

Justin sat there, his shoulders drooping and his eyes upon her, waiting to hear what he knew in his gut was coming next. "Noooo...." he whispered. "It's a lie, Lauren, he's fine. He's just saying that to keep you with him."

Lauren watched with excruciating pain as Justin's face collapsed. His grief was equal to hers. She shook her head. "I can't leave him, Justin. I can't. I married him, for better or worse, in sickness and in health. If I were dying, he would stand by me. He never did anything to deserve my betrayal, Justin. I think I wanted to see it that way because it helped my conscience feel better when I wanted to be with you."

Her voice was soft and her eyes pleading with him to understand.

"But...but...what about us?" he asked, his voice ragged and needing reassurance.

Lauren just looked him straight in the eyes and slowly shook her head. "I'm so sorry," she cried and meant it with every fiber of her being.

"I don't accept it," he said, his voice angry now, in complete denial.

"Justin, please don't make this harder on me than it already is, please?" Lauren begged him.

Justin stopped then and looked at her. His darling Lauren was so filled with confusion and hurt. She loved him, he knew that. But she was an honorable woman and her husband was dying. No matter what she felt for him, Justin knew that looking after her husband was the right thing to do...the only thing to do. His job right now was to make that easier.

It took several long minutes, but then Justin nodded. "I don't want to say it, but I know you're right. Lauren, never, ever, ever forget how much I love you and that will not change. I will always be there...waiting."

She began to cry again, her shoulders quaking with the mixture of regret, longing and relief. He looked at her and never loved her more than in that moment. He would always remember how she looked...her tender skin exposed and covered with rivulets of tears. With resolve, he leaned over her and opened her door. "Go, sweetheart. Go now."

Lauren couldn't even look at Justin. She half slid, half stumbled out of his car and walked toward the front door of her house. She couldn't look back. She heard the car shift into reverse, heard him back up and then drive down the street.

She heard him leave her life.

Weighted down with misery, she went to open her front door, but it opened on its own. She looked up to see Monica standing there.

Monica nodded, "I saw," she said softly. Monica had tears of her own in her eyes. She threw her arms around Lauren and over Monica's shoulder, Lauren could see Nikki, fast asleep on the sofa with an afghan thrown over her naked shoulders. "Let her sleep," Monica whispered and walked Lauren toward the stairway.

Once in Lauren's room, Monica found a nightgown in the drawer and held it out toward Lauren, who put it on mechanically and lay down on the top of the bedclothes. Monica sat down next to her, patting her leg and cooing, "There now...you get some sleep."

Lauren closed her eyes and then a thought suddenly occurred to her. Monica was being too sweet. She looked at Monica and asked softly, "You knew, didn't you?"

Monica hesitated and then slowly nodded. "He told me the day I came to accuse him of fooling around on you. He knew you would need me once you found out, but swore me to secrecy in the meantime."

"No wonder you were so mad," Lauren marveled. "Now I understand."

Monica nodded. "You're seeing him through it, aren't you?"

"Of course," Lauren nodded. "Of course," and then burst into a fresh round of sobbing. Monica kicked off her shoes, slid up onto the bed next to Lauren, wrapped her arm over Lauren's shaking shoulders and stayed there until at long last, they both fell asleep.

CHAPTER FORTY-FIVE

Two weeks later the board sat around the conference table, a somber mood in the air.

Mason Anderson had, indeed, suffered a paralyzing stroke and the fact that treatment was so long delayed awaiting the bariatric gurney factored in. He was unlikely to recover the use of one side of his body, or his speech and there was strong evidence of brain damage from the lack of oxygen. They could not care for him in the regional nursing homes due to his size so he had been sent to Ohio, to a bariatric nursing home that was equipped with lifts and welded, oversized hospital beds.

Despite the fact that Mason was an attorney, he had not taken steps to protect himself financially. He had expected to live forever. As it was, his home, his bank accounts, his vacation cabin, cars...everything, including his share of the law firm, would be liquidated to pay for his care. Once he was broke, it was expected that his care would decline and Mason

Anderson would see the death he had thought would be so long in coming.

So, the task at hand was to select a new captain to take the firm's helm. The members sat around the table, but it was already accepted who would be his successor.

Only Stanley Shore was absent; having suddenly requested an indefinite leave of absence to deal with some personal business. It was not expected that he would return anytime soon. Someone had heard he might even be moving…to Ohio.

"Lauren?" spoke up Jennison, the self-appointed spokesman for the group.

Lauren looked up and saw all eyes on her.

"Lauren, the board has asked me to represent them and to offer you the position recently vacated by Mason Anderson. Your salary would, of course, be the same as his and your shares increased likewise. We are indebted to you, and to Aaron, for keeping the taint of Anderson's actions private; thereby saving the firm and all of our jobs. We feel you are not only eminently qualified, but that you have earned our respect and our gratitude. Do you accept?"

Lauren looked across at Aaron, the tension of the last two weeks only adding to the sallow, loose flesh beneath his eyes. She stood, easing her chair backward, and walked over to the window; the same where she had stood that night, two weeks earlier, when she thought her life was in Anderson's hands.

Justin...was gone. Disappeared without a word. He did not answer the disposable cell phone he had given her, was not at his home and had not even collected his things from the office. It was as if he had never existed. Lauren knew in her heart that his actions were the ultimate proof of his love for her. He had made it easy for her to stay. He knew if he remained, she would constantly be in pain.

She turned now and faced the group. "Gentlemen. I won't lie. I have long coveted the seat at the head of this table. In my eagerness to prove myself, I've taken chances, tolerated behavior I should not have, given loyalty where none was deserved and in general, sold my soul to the devil," she said, motioning to Mason's vacated chair to indicate who she meant.

"The firm of Anderson & Anderson will be better off without Mason Anderson. It will be better off without me." There was a jointly indrawn breath of shock around the table. They had not expected this.

"I am tendering my resignation, as is my husband, Aaron, by the end of business today. It is our intent to take some time off for ourselves, rest and make plans for the next firm we will head, Reynolds & Reynolds."

Another intake of breath; this time of fear and dread as the partners in the room knew who made this firm whole and who would take it down.

"It is my feeling that my husband and I have come to the point in time where we need to separate ourselves from the Anderson name. Perhaps you may even consider changing the firm's name yourselves...something more generic...perhaps 'Boston Legal Associates' would be more in keeping? As for myself, I am honored that you would offer this position to me, and don't think I didn't have to consider this long and hard. However, Aaron and I have things to accomplish that you cannot be a part of, nor can we accomplish these feats while still remaining here.

396

So, it is with regret that I must refuse your offer and wish each and every one of you, success and good health. Oh, and if you're looking for someone to fill in the empty chairs...I believe there is a Mr. Porting who is about to retire form the A.G.'s office and he may be just the man to fit in," she added.

With that, Lauren and Aaron stood, gathered up their tablets and papers and left the room. A few short instructions to Betsy and an hour later, Lauren and Aaron were in his Mercedes, heading for home. They had never felt so free.

Nikki cuddled up against Brad in the double bed at her apartment. They were watching *Sunday Morning* together, mugs of steaming coffee and the Sunday paper completing the tableau upon the bed. On Nikki's left hand glittered a brand new engagement ring; having earned that title only the night before when Brad, only moments before orgasm, had rushed out the words of proposal. Nikki had screamed, "Yes!!!!!" and the neighbors thought once again about installing extra soundproofing on the wall adjoining Nikki's apartment.

"I want a baby," Nikki said suddenly, holding out her hand to let the morning sunlight bounce off the ring in prisms.

"No," Brad said with an air of finality.

"No?" she repeated, her eyes wide in disbelief.

"No," he said again. *We* want a baby," he laughed and she slapped him playfully on the bare ass and instantly fastened her mouth down upon his penis.

"Let's get busy," she said and Brad could offer no resistance to a suggestion so delightfully made.

Morgan was dragging the last of Monica's many boxes back into their house. "How the hell did you get all these out of here without me knowing?" he asked in a mock disgusted voice.

"I didn't," she answered him saucily. "I bought all that stuff new with your credit cards," she said sweetly.

Morgan stopped dead in his tracks. "You did what?" his voice rose until he saw the look on his wife's face. "Okay, but don't buy any more," he ordered, shoving the last box inside the door.

"Not until I'm furnishing a nursery," she said in a playful voice.

"Yeah, yeah, I know," he answered resigned. At least his wife was back in his life and living in their house. Let Monica have her nursery. In the meantime, they were fixing up the spare bedroom for his dad to move in with them. Monica loved the old man and God knows, Morgan could use his father's help in keeping an eye on her and the credit cards.

CHAPTER FORTY-SIX

Endings are often beginnings in disguise...

Sunlight sparkled off the waves and fluttered in through the mullioned windows like butterflies of light. Lauren felt so peaceful.

She and Aaron had left the city and bought a large cottage overlooking the ocean on Cape Cod. It had offered a huge, wrap-around front porch that Lauren had enclosed and now the sign, "Reynolds & Reynolds, Attorneys at Law" graced its door.

Four years earlier, immediately after they had left the firm, their voyage of discovery had begun. Lauren had been at Aaron's side through the many trips to clinics and doctors all over the world. Together they spent long hours researching every possible avenue of treatment for him. He had been subject to special diets, medicinal trials, even treatments using the spectrum of light from a special bulb. He had ingested food grade

400

peroxide and enough organic food to feed a commune for a year.

In France they ate snails and drank wine at cafés that littered sidewalks everywhere. In Switzerland they had boarded a gondola and ridden into the mountain peaks where the air was so clean it almost hurt to inhale it.

By the time they had reached Spain, Lauren began feeling ill. At first she was nauseas and they assumed it was the water or the local food. Alarmed, they boarded a flight for home and took refuge in the yet-to-be completed cottage on the ocean. Later, it became a haven of celebration as Lauren discovered the only thing wrong with her, was that she was pregnant!

Aaron was overjoyed and took up his various alternative treatments with a renewed determination. He knew he would have a son; he could feel it in his bones, as weak as they were.

As Lauren grew plump and then began to resemble the Halloween pumpkins that dotted the neighboring porches, Aaron seemed to grow stronger. He was doing some of the remodeling himself, building a closet into the smaller bedroom so they would have a nursery.

He took up the law again, starting with a few simple divorce cases and then he, with Lauren coaching in the background, took on the defense of a local man, accused of murder. Aaron prevailed and the couple celebrated with tiny sips of champagne. Their firm was off and running!

There was no word from Justin. The firm sent over a courier from time to time, as papers were unearthed that either Lauren or Aaron needed to sign or clarify and each time Lauren managed to quietly ask after Justin. Each time the courier shook his or her head.

Monica and Morgan visited often and seldom came without Nikki and Brad in tow. Nikki was beaming with wedding plans and Monica had taken to carrying a pregnancy test kit in her handbag.

Max David Reynolds was born on a snowy night just before Christmas. Lauren had been feeling different all day and as a first-time mother, she did not know what labor pains would feel like. She thought she might be coming down with a virus, but the cramping was regular at intervals and finally she realized what was going on. She and Aaron climbed into the Mercedes and sped off for the hospital, Lauren texting Monica and Nikki with the impending news as they drove.

Max was born in the wee hours of the morning. His hearty cry could be heard down two hallways and the girls celebrated while Lauren fell into an exhausted sleep.

Aaron stood outside the nursery window for hours until two days later, Max and Lauren were cleared to come home. Aaron adored his son, often setting up a TV tray in the nursery so he could work on papers while the infant slept in the nearby crib. Aaron insisted on taking the night feedings, letting Lauren sleep.

As Max grew, so did the practice. Lauren became an active partner now and her reputation from the big city had preceded her. She was widely sought after and her schedule was full. Betsy had also left the firm and now worked for Lauren and Aaron as legal secretary. They were a family; all of them clustered on the bay with sand dunes in summer and snow-frosted evergreens to carry them through the picturesque winters.

Max was almost four-years-old; a healthy, intelligent toddler who was into everything, when Aaron began to decline in health. His doctors were puzzled and could only guess that he had been running on pure adrenalin those previous four years. While there had been advances in medicine, there was yet no cure. The only option they could offer was a sort of modified blood transplant. Healthy blood was processed and boosted and then introduced into his body in ever-increasing amounts over a short period of time. The result was that the recipient's own body should identify the powered formula and begin reproducing the healthy cells at a greater rate than their unhealthy counterparts.

All that was needed was a donor; and it must be an exact match. The only place to find this would be from his own son's cord blood, something that Lauren had taken the precaution of having frozen and stored since Max's birth. It was an experimental procedure and a slim hope; yet it was the only hope they had.

Lauren went to the repository where Max's cord blood was stored and signed a release. It was sent to the clinic where Aaron was being treated, to be tested and matched.

Aaron had been hospitalized in the clinic for over a week now and his strength was rapidly declining. He could no longer bear the weight of Max on his bed, for the toddler moved about a great deal and Aaron simply did not have the strength to prevent him from falling, or even the weight of Max's tiny head lying on his chest in love. It was a heartbreaking sight and Lauren considered not bringing Max to the clinic any longer. There was, however, no way to know when it would be too late to change her mind.

Lauren got a phone call from the clinic that Aaron's doctor wanted to talk to her. She had just filed some papers in the local courthouse and called Betsy to stay with Max until she could get home.

She found Dr. Wilson in his tiny cubicle office that overlooked a park where the more ambulatory patients could be wheeled around in the fresh air. He was seated in a high back leather chair and had a solemn look on his face when she was ushered in.

Lauren knew without a word what he was going to say. "It won't work?" she asked without preamble.

"Mrs. Reynolds, the blood does not match." He delivered the crushing words without expression. He was a trained professional who was accustomed to the harsher sides of living.

"How can that be? How could Max's blood not match Aaron's?" Almost as soon as she said the words, the blood drained from her face and she knew the answer.

"Mrs. Reynolds, I'm sorry to say this and while I don't need to know the details, I have to assure you that we're 100% certain that Max is not Aaron's biological child. I'm sorry...but there's nothing we can do."

Lauren stood mechanically and her lack of response told the doctor exactly what he had guessed. Aaron Reynolds was raising another man's son.

The end